A NOVEL BY GURASIS KAUR

MORE THAN*
~~Just~~ Friends?

BlueRose ONE
Stories Matter
New Delhi • London

BLUEROSE PUBLISHERS
India | U.K.

Copyright © Gurasis kaur 2024

All rights reserved by author. No part of this publication may be reproduced, stored in a retrieval system or transmitted in any form or by any means, electronic, mechanical, photocopying, recording or otherwise, without the prior permission of the author. Although every precaution has been taken to verify the accuracy of the information contained herein, the publisher assumes no responsibility for any errors or omissions. No liability is assumed for damages that may result from the use of information contained within.

BlueRose Publishers takes no responsibility for any damages, losses, or liabilities that may arise from the use or misuse of the information, products, or services provided in this publication.

For permissions requests or inquiries regarding this publication, please contact:

BLUEROSE PUBLISHERS
www.BlueRoseONE.com
info@bluerosepublishers.com
+91 8882 898 898
+4407342408967

ISBN: 978-93-6452-882-5

Cover design: Shivani
Typesetting: Sagar

First Edition: August 2024

Dedication

To people who believe that love is not a chapter they could close,
But a complete story they would re-read
Let's make a deal,
You would be the author here and someone you love will lead.

Contents

Chapter 1

Did it end?... 1

Chapter 2

Stepping into Riva's shoes for a day 10

Chapter 3

An addition maybe?...22

Chapter 4

Hooked up? Seriously?...32

Chapter 5

'US' is what all i need...42

Chapter 6

I am proud of you, abir!..50

Chapter 7

Turned upside down 65

Chapter 8

Half semester only/- 73

Chapter 9

Dreadful dinner..82

Chapter 10th:

Confusion, confusion everywhere.
Not a single brain cell to think. 93

Chapter 11

Corporate girlie tryna balance life with love.................100

Chapter 12

Let me comfort you..114

Chapter 13

Approaching the end?...122

Chapter 14

Birthday bash babe. 126

Chapter 15

And yes, a date...135

Chapter 16

Did it start?..153

Acknowledgement 159

About the author: 160

About the editor 161

Chapter 1

Did it end?

"I was very sure that something wrong was about to occur because a lot of right things had happened."

"Why does everything that starts to feel so right end so badly?" Saharanpur had been one of my favorite destinations throughout the school years. My Naani lived there, and I used to visit her frequently during my high school days. I had made many friends there, and Ankush was one of them. We had been dating for two years. He lived next door to my Naani, and no one in my family knew about our relationship. I had become adept at keeping things private. This started when I once lied to them about passing in exam, later I re-appeared for the same subject, and none in my family got to know about it. So that incident made me believe in my abilities to keep things private. Like other children, my equation with my parents, especially mom was not that good. She always appeared strict with academics and career, so never discussed about boys with her. Anyways, Ankush had always been a significant figure in my life, my first love. As I continued to visit Saharanpur more often, our relationship deepened.

I still remember the first time I entered his home; he had greeted me with a rose and oil was spread on one side of the floor to welcome me. *'This is how we welcome someone special in our tradition,' he smiled. I entered, took the rose from his hand, and replied, 'This is how we embrace special treatment in our tradition.'*

You might be wondering why a grade twelfth student would need to tell her mother a falsehood about something so elementary. But it wasn't always easy to get along with my mother, Sneha. Our different expectations have been one of the main causes of my stress. She wanted me to secure rank one in major arenas of my life ranging from academics to only academics. Nevertheless, the more she pressured me to work hard and excel, the more average I ended up in my studies. There were times of self-doubt and self-guilt as well but by God's grace I had wonderful friends who helped me cope with it.

Things were going well until I began visiting Saharanpur three times a month. Sadly, my Naani passed away due to a cardiac stroke, while I was preparing for my board exams and everything abruptly changed. I no longer had a compelling reason to visit the city so frequently. Additionally, my mother, who had a strained relationship with her brother, made it unequivocal by saying, 'Visits to Saharanpur are now over.'

I recall a year ago, as we concluded my Naani's funeral rites, the moment for everyone to depart arrived. In one of the quieter corners, Ankush approached me and said, "I understand it might not be the appropriate time to ask, but I've been wondering if you plan to visit here again after this."

"My mother believes we have no reason to stay here now. Even Maama and Maami won't summon us," I responded with a heavy heart, without looking into his beautiful eyes.

"What about you? You still have your connections here, right? You can always use Virat as a reason." Ankush was clearly anxious at the thought of me not visiting Saharanpur anymore and I couldn't bear the sadness in his voice that I was the reason of.

"You very well know that my parents are not aware of the fact that Virat and I share a good cousin bond. He never told Maami that we used to hang out or bunk classes together. She would have killed him. Please try to understand, I have a very complex family; things aren't sorted here. Give me some space." With this, I left without turning back because I couldn't face him anymore almost after breaking his heart. Also, deep down I had an intuition that somebody had overheard us. I couldn't figure out whom, but somebody definitely did. After we concluded the rituals, mom asked me to pack my stuff.

Soon we returned to Delhi, and I had begun my normal routine. Starting a long-distance relationship appeared doable; yet sustaining it became the real challenge. Oddly enough, we never experienced any arguments, and perhaps that's where our problems arose. A quarrel might have resolved our misunderstandings, dispelling unnecessary doubts, and figuring things out. But even an argument demands time that we couldn't spare for each other. Our daily schedules were significantly different due to our college routines. But, we managed to keep things going for another year, and then came the day when my life changed. On August 14th, came in a brand-new chapter in our love story namely cheating douchebag or heartbreak, whatever you like to call it.

It was on this day when my mom and I were going to Saharanpur for some property-related issues. I had decided to surprise Ankush and expected the day to be golden for both of us. We were supposed to meet exactly after a year of Naani's death and I knew that the reunion would be quite peaceful, exciting and healer for our relationship. To know about his whereabouts, I texted Gaurav, Ankush's best friend, asking for a meet-up to surprise Ankush.

"Oh, you are in town!?" He responded excitedly.

"Yes, I thought you, me, and Ankush could meet for a while and watch Netflix and chill at your place like we used to do earlier."

"Sure, let's catch up tomorrow. Not today because, Ankush had gone to Aarvi's birthday. I don't think he would return before midnight."

"Aarvi? Who's she?"

"After you left the city permanently, she approached him, and as far as I think, they are getting quite serious with each other now. Please don't tell him that I told you this." Gaurav's text left me utterly speechless.

The train came to an abrupt halt, and for a brief moment, so did my heartbeat. I couldn't concentrate on my mother's words, the complaints from fellow passengers disturbed by my presence, the weight of a bag that had fallen on my foot, or even the incessant crying of a baby. It all froze in time. While I had a strong urge to confide in my best friends, Riva and Abir,

I chose to initiate my investigation first. I couldn't simply depend on someone else's accusations of my boyfriend cheating on me.

I understood that the past one year had been exceptionally challenging for both of us, but the thought of moving on never crossed my mind. One part of me found it hard to believe that Ankush could be unfaithful, while the other part pondered why his best-friend would fabricate such a story. It made me reflect on whether this was the real reason why Ankush had always been reluctant for Gaurav to know about our relationship, maintaining a noticeable distance between us. While I couldn't comprehend his motives, I felt an urgent need to connect the dots and seek clarity from him as soon as possible.

"Hey, are you there?" When a message appeared, I realized I had been conversing with Gaurav.

"Oh yes, I was just wondering if Ankush had ever told me about any Aarvi or not?"

"That's a dumb question. Why would you need Ankush to tell you about her? She has been your Mama's tenant for a few months. I thought you must have known her."

"Well, Maama doesn't disclose such details. Anyway, let them have their café dates. We can meet up later," I added with a subtle emphasis on 'café' to prompt the actual location.

'Café? No, Ankush is actually at Aarvi's apartment. She has hosted a house party,'

As we had reached the station and booked a cab to the final destination, I lied to my mom about Daisy constantly asking to meet her first. Rather, I immediately proceeded upstairs, sprinted, two at a time, where the tenants were meant to reside. While ringing the doorbell, I shuddered, and my eyes began to well up. My brain sensed something was amiss, yet I prayed for things to remain positive.

A girl continued to stare at me when the door opened. She matched her light pink crop top and pink heels with a bright pink bag.

Who could be this pink? ugh.

Nevertheless, I questioned her if she was Aarvi. She shook her head and told me that she was Geetanshi, Aarvi's friend.

"Oh, I am... I am Ananya. I had come to wish her a very happy birthday! May I?"

"Oh, just a second." With this, I encountered three guys accompanied by three girls. My gaze was searching for Ankush, and the people around me grew curious about my presence. Aarvi took a step closer and began to express her suspicions. I wondered whether she had seen me before or if Ankush had mentioned something about her to me.

"I am sorry to disturb your event. This is my mama's place, and he asked me to wish you a very happy birthday. I just came for that. Well, It's a great party, have a great celebration." I wanted to inquire if Ankush was present, but I couldn't muster up the courage to do so. Perhaps I wasn't emotionally prepared to hear any negative update. When I failed to spot him, I managed to convince myself that Gaurav had been dishonest. I contemplated leaving, but then...

"This Zomato guy is not picking up the phone, baby. What should we...?"

I turned, and just simply lost control. It was none other than Ankush. My boyfriend, my first love for whom I had started developing feelings, for whom I had prepared a surprise...well, guess who got the surprise instead! I stared at him, leaving everyone confused.

"Do you guys know each other?" Aarvi questioned me.

"You better ask him." I snapped.

"Ana, please don't create a fuss. We will talk about this later." *The balls of him.*

I was fuming and there he was looking into my eyes and convincing me to not create a fuss on his supposedly *baby's* birthday.

"Enough with your 'later.' Talk to me now. I don't have time for your nonsense. Do you think this is how you build a beautiful long-distance relationship? Give me a break. I've been shouldering the blame for all the issues in our relationship, but at least I've remained faithful. That's the least you could do for someone. Riva kept on warning me to withdraw from this emotionally disturbing not-so-peaceful relationship, but I still stood there! And you? Dating two girls at once. Ananya from Delhi and Aarvi from town! What a life, dude!" I yelled.

"What did you just say? Emotionally disturbing relationship? My foot! I gave you the space you always wanted; I gave you the time to process things out, barely ever fought with you so that you won't feel that distance is overpowering us. But if this is what you give in return, just back the hell off from my life!" He yelled it back.

His words seemed poisonous to me. I decided to leave until Aarvi tried to stop me.

"And as for you, Aarvi, if by any chance you were aware that Ankush had a girlfriend and still chose to date him, girl, it's time to raise your standards. I had no intention of ruining your birthday, but if I did, you can thank your 'wonderful' guy!" I snapped at her as well and left.

What a relief it was! Letting it all out, yelling out everything I had pent up for so long, and, most importantly, being completely unfiltered. That's where authentic catharsis lies. I wept for hours, locking myself away, at times in the bathroom, at times behind the doors, and sometimes hidden behind the curtains. It felt even more struggling because I was not in my town. I tried hard to not let Sneha or anyone else found about this chaos. When it turned midnight and everyone else slept, I had called Riva.

"So, how was the surprise?"

"You mean a shock?" I said.

"Oh, so was he cheating on you?"

"You are a real combination of being so accurate and chill, how?"

"It's natural for men to lie. I'm not sure what led you to believe that he had an X factor. Regardless of how lovely your partner is, long-distance relationships are never rewarding. We are just college freshers now, isn't it too early to think of such serious relationships?" She laughed a little.

"I don't get it. Once I return to Delhi, the three of us will meet and then talk about it." I hung up the phone and had texted Virat that I was not feeling good. He immediately showed up to my room with a pair of cigarettes and half bottled beer to ease my sadness. He noticed that Ankush and I had some unresolved issues. When I confided in him about everything, he seemed perplexed. He had never seen Ankush at the apartment before and urged me to investigate further, but I declined.

"What's gone is gone. Why would I scratch this topic anymore? These few months have taught me how to live without this relationship. I don't need him." I had cried harder.

We stayed up late that night, talking about how HE could do that to me and that I won't say a yes to any long distance relationship ever! Next morning, while I tried to get back to my conscious, I overheard an argument between my mom and her brother. So I went to see her and she was engrossed in her paperwork and asked me to pick up some essentials from a nearby grocery store as we were supposed to leave in a few hours.

After I got done with the task, Sneha booked a cab to the railway station, as we were preparing to depart for Delhi. The distinct feeling this time was the certainty that after this journey, there would be no compelling reason to return. I gave a side hug to Virat, bidding farewell to everyone. It turned into a profoundly emotional moment. Even the elders shared heartfelt goodbyes, and I returned to Delhi with a heavy heart.

"I wonder if I would ever get the strength to unlock some of my emotions"

Chapter 2

Stepping into Riva's shoes for a day

It was an early Monday morning when the three of us—Abir, Riva, and I—decided to bunk our fourth lecture and meet at the same stall we had been gathering at for the past two semesters, *'YUM-YUM MORE.'*

"Let's welcome the 'Sad freak!' of the day - Ana, who has recently experienced heartbreak!" Riva exclaimed.

"What the fuck, Shut up!" I retorted.

"Wait, I think you're jumping to conclusions. You should talk to Ankush once. I'm not defending him, but I think things shouldn't be ruined like this," Abir interrupted.

"I've blocked him everywhere. I don't feel like I need him in my life anymore. Moreover it's like I can finally breathe and I don't need to have constant niggling of my so called "Relationship" Besides, I'd rather prefer reading old chats rather than speaking to him. Because even if he turns out to be right, what would I do then? I'm not prepared for another long-distance relationship," I explained.

"That's the crux of it. You're simply using an excuse to keep your distance from him. Deep down, you realize there's a chance you might be mistaken, and he could be in the right, but you're concerned about how to navigate this relationship, aren't you?" Abir nodded in agreement. I smiled, pretending to peruse the menu and fiddle with the glasses needlessly just to keep my hands busy. Abir's words held a certain truth to them, something I might have been avoiding. He arched an eyebrow, but I remained lost in thought.

DAMN IT. I HATE IT WHEN HE IS RIGHT.

Abir has been my closest friend since 9th grade, and no one knew me as well as he did. From our early days learning to ride bicycles together to enjoying long car rides, we had experienced it all. We even used to share the same lunchboxes, and only he could accurately guess the exact type of noodles I craved. Whenever we went out for lunch, he would place a special order for me, bake delicious cookies, and surprise me with thoughtful gestures. His jokes could be teasing, but he never allowed anyone else to say a word against me. He was always been a shining light in my darkness or a constant whenever I felt deflated. Indeed, true guy best friends are priceless.

"Wait; let's just drop a clarification now. ANKUSH'S CHAPTER IS OVER FOR REAL." Riva said.

"Yaar, life would be so boring now. I don't want this breakup to ruin my college life. I have been dealing with issues with Sneha, and just when I thought I could escape the toxicity at home, another disaster struck. It's like I'm caught in a never-ending storm. What am I even doing?" I chuckled bitterly.

"Could you ever just call your mom respectfully?" Abir interrupted.

"Why should I? Not everyone had that luxury to have a mom who would chop someone's head if they messed with their kid", I said flicking my gaze to him. But hey, you wouldn't understand the pain, my voice tinged with frustration and hurt.

"Listen up! How about you step into my shoes for a month? No heavy relationships, no commitments, no complications! The only thing on your agenda would be having fun. You're free to go on blind dates, share a passionate kiss with a handsome stranger, and then forget him the very next day as if he never existed. And just like they say, the best way to move on is to move to someone new.

Believe me, casual dates provide far more memorable moments and smiles as compared to serious, suffocating relationships." She exclaimed in joy.

Abir didn't like Riva's idea. He looked disappointed, but he nodded anyway. It seemed like he was worried about me and where this idea might take us. We have always been close friends, sticking together through thick and thin. Riva's suggestion was taking us into new and unknown territory. At first, I was hesitant to follow up because hook-up culture was never my forte; but eventually, she persuaded me to at least give the fun a shot. I began to consider that it wouldn't be a bad idea to temporarily put myself in her position. The three of us continued with our snacks until Sneha called up.

God is seriously pissed at me.

"Please stay quiet, it's Sneha calling!" Then least heartedly, I picked up the call.

"Yes Mom, I am in the middle of a lecture. I will call you as soon as I get free." I was about to hang up the phone when she told me about the surprise guest appearance at our place for dinner. My dad had invited his friend and his wife for lunch. Mom requested me to come a little early so that I could help her with the preparations. After we wrapped up the meal, Abir brought up an internship that seemed interesting to him.

"I am not looking for an internship as of now. Please keep your academic side separated when you meet us!" I laughed.

"Alright, if you're not interested here, how about exploring content writing? I've read your quotes; they're amazing! You should nurture that talent. If I had your skill, trust me, I wouldn't let it go to waste." He suggested.

I nodded and gave him a sarcastic smile, telling him that I was in Riva's bubble then.

The world has three kinds of people: one who does not believe in you, one who believes in you, and then come those who make you believe in yourself. Abir was one of them. I knew that even if the whole world, including my mom, would sneer me for being an average student in studies and accomplishing nothing in life, Abir would still be there praising my little achievements.

It's how he is. Always seeing the best in people and supporting them through and through. He would literally destroy himself to protect his loved ones. In between the conversation, he got a call from his mother, and excused us. While Riva and I were chilling and having drinks together, she broke the silence and said,

"Listen, I understand this is tough for you. But sometimes, what appears challenging is essential. I've witnessed your struggles with Ankush's chapter, and I genuinely want to spare you that pain again. Let it remain in the past. You must rekindle your spirit now. Our world embraces casual dating, just being in flings, where there are no expectations. It might be something you'd enjoy experiencing as me." Her words convinced me that long-distance relationships rarely yield positive outcomes. Engaging in a committed relationship often brings forth conflicts, disputes, and constraints. On the contrary, indulging in no string arrangement can bring happiness, laughter, and what some might term a heightened sense of intimacy. I think that's what I really need. A break from my old self and be a free bird.

Abir needed a ride home, so he asked if I could join him. I agreed and wished Riva luck with her last lecture. I insisted her to come along as well, but Abir, speaking on her behalf, said, "It's fine; let her at least secure the minimum attendance." I missed this, the light teasing, drama-free life and moreover, the comfort of my friends. They were my RIDE or DIE. Up until this point, I didn't even realise what I was missing out on but being with them for a handful of hours and I was already feeling light as a balloon.

We left the place and soon found ourselves stuck in traffic near NSP. The heat was unbearable, and unfortunately, the car's AC wasn't functioning due to technical issues.

"It's hot today, isn't it?" Abir remarked as he wiped the sweat from his face. I burst into laughter and teased, "Only because you let such hotness travel with you." He blushed slightly, and I continued to playfully tease him. Before he could drop me off at home, he brought up the topic of content writing again.

"Abir, I don't think I'm cut out for it. Only you truly understand the meaning behind my seemingly foolish quotes. Remember all those poetry competitions in school? I always came back with just a participation certificate. I don't have the confidence for it right now. Let's drop this discussion," I said.

Meanwhile, my mom was calling impatiently, asking where I was. I picked up the phone and told her not to bother me like this, explaining that I'd be home in a few minutes.

"You know, a simple apology would have fixed everything. Or even better, not an apology, but some ice cream could make amends now. Get some for everyone and tell them the vendor was slow. At least that way, they won't scold you," Abir suggested as soon as I ended the call.

Yes, that's him. Always the good kid with a brat aka me.

"Sneha is going to mad at me now! But, I'm always prepared for it." I chuckled.

"It's not about that. I just don't want anyone else to scold or yell at you, except for ME." he winked.

"Why, do you think you're so special?"

"Am I not?"

His abrupt question caught me off guard and I don't know why I was feeling suddenly extremely hot in the car. Why the hell is this AC not working?

"Haha, you're incredibly special. You mean the world to me, my dearest friend. While there may be casual flings and perks on one side, having you by my side on the other, our bond is truly unparalleled." I smiled and gave him a reassuring bond.

My connection with him was truly remarkable. We started as school buddies and became the closest friends in college. You know like from sandbox to casket types. Many in the college assumed that we were dating. For those who believe that a guy and a girl can't be best friends, they just need to look at us. We've frequented numerous cafes, argued over whom should foot the bill, have pulled countless pranks, and created a wealth of cherished memories together. Our friendship was so tight that whenever Abir was running late, the first person his mom would text was me, checking if he was with me or not. We have always been each other's safe place but never crossed the line.

We were partners in crime not in bed. Wait, what? Why am I even thinking about bed? And also, Abir in the same sentence? God, I am truly fucked up with this break-up.

He dropped me near the colony gate and I made my way to my home. As I entered my apartment, I noticed the guests engaged in lively conversation while enjoying samosas and dhoklas. *What an unusual combination.*

Then, my gaze locked onto one of the most attractive guys there, Sameer. He seemed like a fitness enthusiast; his muscles were clearly defined beneath his snug shirt, veins visible through his partially rolled-up sleeves, and his smile was captivating. From a certain angle, he looked every bit like a celebrity, and I couldn't take my eyes off him.

After taking off my shoes, I joined the gathering in the living room, where my father introduced me to everyone.

"Oh, you're in your third year, that's fantastic. Sameer is currently preparing for his sixth-semester exams. He is half a semester ahead of you," his dad struck up a conversation.

"Yes, uncle, I will be having my fifth-semester exams very soon. The rest I haven't thought about yet. And you?" I raised my eyebrows towards Sameer.

"I haven't thought about it yet too." he smiled.

He looked so attractive while nodding. Moreover, his voice was incredibly appealing. As our conversation continued, my mom requested to pick up some groceries from the nearby store. I was about to grab the keys to my two-wheeler when Sameer's mom won my heart with her suggestion.

"Why don't you take him along too? What would you two do amidst our boring adult conversation, right?" she said. *Can I kiss her for this?*

I couldn't express how grateful I felt to her. Sameer got up and asked if I knew how to drive. I playfully winked at him and replied, "I'm quite skilled at it."

We embarked on a scooty ride, and I showed him to our former residence, my former school, and a sprawling nearby park. We were enjoying ourselves when, all of a sudden, the scooty came to a halt. I initially thought we had run out of petrol, but it turned out to be a different problem. We made our way to a nearby mechanic for assistance. I had already informed Sneha about the situation, so it was just Sameer and me, walking along a dimly lit street, observing the mechanic, and trying to ease the awkward silence that hung between us.

"So you are doing computer science, right?" I tried breaking the ice.

"Yes, and you are doing BBA from MKL college, my dad told me."

I simply nodded and welcomed the once again silence but then his question pulled me shockingly from my thoughts. "By the way, do you have a boyfriend?" Sameer asked me, and as the words left his lips, a sudden shyness overcame him. He nervously started rubbing his hand and attempted to change the topic. I explained about my recent 'ex' relationship and how my perspective on relationships had evolved since then. He was genuinely interested in hearing the whole story, so he suggested we head to a nearby park. I agreed, and we entered the tranquil greenery of the deer park.

We located a bench, which was rather small, yet we managed to squeeze onto it instead of searching for another spot. He sat very close to me, and his scent was undeniably enticing. As I began to share a bit about Ankush, he kept on nodding and showed curiosity to listen more. Within a few minutes, we started to vibe, exchanged smiles with each-other and had a good time together. Soon, we noticed a couple kissing in front of us, which left both of us feeling somewhat flustered.

"Well, it's common in this park, not in this locality, I mean," I murmured.

"I think it should be common everywhere, right?" He winked.

Woah, that's some, flirting.

"Okay, so you are saying that the act of kissing should be normalized in public places."

"No, I am only saying that acts of kissing should be normalized. The place doesn't matter. PDA's should be normal."

"Oh, the partner matters?" I sounded confused.

"No, the time, the mood, and the intensity matters," he said with deep gaze on me and in a totally serious note.

I sensed all the signals that he was eager to make a move. To be honest, I was inclined to reciprocate. I had already decided that I wouldn't see him again after this, so trying a kiss with him didn't seem like a bad idea. Lost in my contemplation, I failed to notice him drawing nearer, and he leaned in slightly. I closed my eyes, parted my lips and just like that, I shared my first kiss with a stranger I had known for just a few minutes. *Oops, was it childish?* Well, undeniably intriguing, to say the least. After all, it was Riva's reflection in me.

We paused after the initial kiss, locking eyes with one another. There was no one else around, and we were completely absorbed in each other's gaze. Without hesitation, we continued kissing for a solid five minutes before I decided it was time to stop. I sensed him attempting to explore further, deepening the kiss and slipping his hand inside my shirt, but I wasn't ready for that. Respectful of my boundaries, he ceased. We decided to stop, and I asked him to check for the mechanic. We retrieved the scooty and brought the groceries. Upon returning home, Sameer's mom gifted me a pair of lipsticks, and I expressed my gratitude for the thoughtful gifts. After having the last drinks, the guests were preparing to leave, and my parents accompanied them downstairs for the final goodbye. I stayed in the kitchen, tidying up when suddenly Sameer entered.

"What happened?"

"Nothing, Dad just left his keys here. Shall I pick them up?" he said.

"Oh, sure. By the way, say thanks to your mom again, I like these lipsticks," I smiled.

"Well, the one that you have put on also seems nice. Wish I could taste it again," Sameer remarked, his banter never failing to make me blush and laugh simultaneously. In response, I playfully dropped the box and moved closer to him. Leaning in, I brushed my lips on his ear and whispered, "No," followed by a teasing laugh, then suggested he should leave.

"After this, neither you nor I will cross each-other's path, right? So, what's the harm in trying it again, Ananya?" Sameer's words, when he used my name for the first time, were incredibly enticing. My ethical reservations were momentarily set aside; I leaned in and kissed him passionately. We were so absorbed in the moment that we forgot people were waiting for him downstairs. It wasn't until the doorbell rang that we reluctantly pulled apart.

Later, I called Abir to update him with the juicy update.

"Hi, There?" I said.

"Hi, what happened? You sound so nervous."

"Well, I have some crazy news to spill. I had my first kiss with Sameer. I mean not the first, of course, but the first after Ankush, yes. Remember I mentioned those guests coming over to my place? Well, he was there, and let me tell you, he's quite a hottie!"

"Whoa, hold on a second! Did you kiss a random guy? Why wasn't I there, man?" He chuckled but I could hear the irritation in his words with my ears closed right now, which was strange.

"Stop teasing, please! But yeah, it was an interesting experience. Oh, and you know what, I always thought that Ankush's thoughts would haunt me, but trust me, I didn't even think of him once while I was kissing him. I want to move on now! And stepping into Riva's shoe was not so bad I think."

Abir didn't respond much and a little awkwardness occurred between us so I decided to end the conversation there. "Let's put that aside. Let bygones be bygones. I need to feel free now. I am hanging up the call now, we will catch up tomorrow."

Pouring your heart out to people you trust, what could be a better feeling than this?

Chapter 3

An addition maybe?

"Wow, you look amazing!" Riva exclaimed as she caught sight of me in a black kurti paired with blue baggy jeans and minimal accessories. I rarely wore ethnic attire to college, but that choice for the day would surely have pleased my mom, who always urged me to dress more traditionally. That is why I always felt that our definitions of everything, whether it was fashion or food, never quite aligned. Just like any other teenage girl, I often concealed my tank top beneath a jacket or wore stockings when leaving home, only to get rid of them later. In fact, thrice in my life, I have changed my entire outfit at Riva's place. Such a clumsy life I had.

"I might be going out this Sunday with my cousins to Iscon. Lend me this attire then," she added.

"This Sunday? Three of us were supposed to head to Adventure Park which is newly opened near our campus, remember?" Abir jumped into the conversation.

"I am sorry, guys, but trust me, you two need not cancel this plan because of me. You guys can have fun. I know you and Ana were excited about it!"

Just as we were trying to make sense of our current situation, a fellow student hurried over to us, bearing news that Professor Saloni Chawla was about to begin a special seminar for BBA students. Although Professor Chawla was renowned for her exceptional teaching of abnormal psychology, her popularity extended beyond the boundaries of the psychology department, as she frequently organized competitions and offered valuable career counselling and motivational lectures to students from various disciplines with a teaching style that was nothing short of phenomenal.

The three of us wasted no time and promptly made our way to meet her. To our surprise, when we arrived at her seminar, we were greeted by a substantial crowd that had gathered to attend the session.

"All of you will soon be taking your fifth-semester exams, and afterward, some of you may seek opportunities beyond our campus. However, as your mentor, I believe it's my responsibility to provide you with a chance to explore your talents. This year, for the entire BBA department, we have introduced a program called 'YBYS' – You Bring Your Own Spark. We are offering Anthology, portrait making, and photography, which are three of the most underrepresented fields on our campus. I truly believe that delving into these areas will enrich our overall learning experience," she explained.

"Ma'am, could you please clarify what exactly we'll be doing in this program?" one of the students inquired.

"For the Anthology project, we are giving you a generous timeframe of three semesters. You can collaborate with a partner and create something creatively compelling. Upon graduation, you'll submit a hard copy of your work. We'll archive them in the college library, and the most appreciated piece will be recognized at next year's festival, attended by esteemed guests," she elaborated.

"As for photography, before you graduate, you'll need to submit a photo story on the topic 'Media Breaks the Privacy.' Collect as many relevant images as you can and weave them into a compelling narrative. The best submission will receive a cash prize of 10,000 rupees."

"Lastly, for portrait making, eligibility is limited to students in art clubs. You'll be given a topic on the spot and allotted 4 hours to create your masterpiece within the college premises. The top three artists will have the opportunity to represent us at the National Art Festival in connaught place, where you'll be required to deliver a captivating speech about your work. The prizes there are truly exceptional. Not to forget that this will happen in the fifth semester itself."

Before we could fully grasp her announcement, Abir's enthusiasm bubbled over, and he began earnestly urging Riva and me to participate. Initially, we declined, but later, we discovered that he had already included my name for the Anthology competition. I made every effort to convey to him that I didn't believe I was a suitable candidate, given my past experiences of rejection during my school years. However, he persistently encouraged me to give it a try at least once.

"Ana, you have almost one year to complete this project. Something remarkable could transpire by then, trust me!" he said with no such a pause. He was excited for me more than for himself.

"Remarkable? Really?" I chuckled softly.

The three of us made our way to the canteen, trying to complete the discussion about the adventure park. I was gently pushing Riva to consider some adjustments to her plan, but she remained resolute. A hint of frustration slipped from her lips, leaving me momentarily stunned.

"Oh, come on. Do you really think I'm cancelling this plan? Just ask Abir! He won't be available after 2 o'clock next Sunday either."

A sense of something secretive passed between them, casting an awkward vibe over the conversation. I turned to Abir, seeking clarification on Riva's statement. Finally, he revealed that he had an appointment at Oberoi Immigration Consultancy. I hesitantly probed further, questioning his motive, and that's when he disclosed his plan to pursue a master's degree in Canada. Initially, I suspected he might be joking, but the confirmation from Riva left me surprised.

"Riva knew this, but I didn't. May I ask why you kept it from me?" I said my voice was deeply graved with hurt or mainly disappointment. Disappointment because I was his best friend, how could he not tell me first and hurt because, *I don't know, how am I going to live without him if he leaves for Canada? How can he decide to leave me here?*

"I don't know. I mean I know, I know that you will jump out of joy knowing that I won't be there to annoy you anymore, and I...I..was simply not wanting you to feel free from my stupidity."

"Abir, this statement must have sound way better in your head but trust me, it sounded so stupid to me. Kindly shutup."

Without a second thought, I aimlessly left the canteen and went to the library. There I closed my eyes and bowed my head down on the table. The only thought that started to bother me was, 'Would he be going abroad?' Will he miss me? He is out there but I am already having a nearly panic attack after the news, what will happen when he really leaves? And why am I so hurt and beyond frustrated with this news? *Because you like him*. Yes, I like him as a friend but this inner turmoil is making me sick to the core and has never happened before even when I was with Ankush.

I was realizing how special Abir was. He might not have opened the car door for me, but he always made sure that I wore my seatbelt even for short trips. He never dedicated a romantic song to me, but I knew he secretly carried me in his art. He was never jealous of me making new friends but never failed to mark his permanent presence no matter what the situation was. Sometimes, I couldn't help but wonder, was he more than just my guy best friend?

A sudden jolt broke me from my thoughts when the librarian came and told me that resting my head was not something acceptable in the library. I left my spot and spotted the two of them having brownies with ice cream, I decided to join in.

"You guys are so mean, having this without me?" I said.

"I tried calling you twice, but it said you were unreachable," Riva replied.

I ignored that constant pit of anxiety and pull up the big girl pants as I asked him. "Anyway, when are you planning to move to Canada? Please let me know beforehand so I can compile a list of things I'd love you to bring back for me."

"Ana, I know you might be upset, but..." he said without so much looking to me.

"I'm not! Why would I be? At least one of us in this trio is achieving success. I'm genuinely thrilled for you. I said giving the best fake smile I could.

"Somebody once said, 'It's an incredible feeling to see a friend settle down and start a new life,' but doesn't that feeling also come with a sense of worry? Knowing that what often accompanies settling down is the growing distance between you and them. Was I prepared for it?

Once we finished our meal, I caught up with Saloni Ma'am, and she reminded me about the Anthology competition, emphasizing the need to take it seriously. Abir attempted to strike up a conversation while also inquiring about the portrait-making competition date. She kindly assured him not to worry and advised him to practice, as the competition was likely to take place in the coming week.

Later, we decided it was time to head back to our homes. Fortunately, Abir had his car with him, and we decided to accompany him.

"You know, Ana, it's because of you that I travel an extra half-hour in the opposite direction to get home," he chuckled.

"Of course, you do! You have no other choice," I teased, winking.

"Oh my goodness, Ana! Look who's taken an interest in you! It's Advait Trehan from English Honors. He must have seen you at the seminar today and is now inquiring about you. He's really hot," Riva interrupted, flashing her phone in front of my face.

"Stop it, Riva. Ana has moved on from your shoe," Abir chimed in, displaying his protective side.

And did I sense jealousy?

I remained quiet, just smiling at his possessiveness. I tried to calm Riva down, explaining that I wasn't interested in anyone at the moment. After all, the semester fifth exams were approaching, and I didn't want to give my mom another reason to throw tantrums at me.

"Riva, you're shaping a mini version of yourself within her," he remarked with the growl of frustration as he lowered the music volume."

"Hey, relax, bro. Why are you getting so worked up? This is a conversation between me and Ananya, right?" she responded.

"Fine, go ahead and form a duo within this trio. It seems that's what you're up to," Abir retorted.

"Now, that's pretty harsh. Just because you don't have any relationships in your life doesn't mean you should discourage us from discussing them," she replied, her tone becoming increasingly irritated.

"I never said that. In fact, I don't want to say anything anymore. You can carry on with your conversation," he stated, raising the music volume in an attempt to put an end to the discussion. However, Riva was not someone to be trifled with. Without wasting a moment, she demanded him to stop the car and promptly exited. She was the fiery element in our trio, capable of blazing with intensity and then returning to her normal self in the blink of an eye.

After she exited the car, I assured Abir that I would talk to her and ask her to apologize as well. She went a little too personal with him, which was certainly inappropriate. While he tried letting me know that he was fine, I knew deep down he was really hurt and disappointed with Riva's words.

Ten minutes later I had almost reached the main entrance of my society, so I decided to say goodbye to him. Immediately after I got out, I dialed Riva's number until I mistakenly bumped into Kartik – a past figure. We used to be real buddies till class 8th, and I had a big friend circle in the society for whom I used to fight with my mom to let me play during the evenings. It was after the 8th that everything changed; all of us got way too busy in our lives, and he too left society and shifted somewhere else with family.

"Oh my God! Is this you, Ana?"

"And you, K...Kartik?" I asked almost stuttering.

"Hell yes! What a pleasant surprise it is to meet you like this. I feel so nostalgic!"

"Me too! The last time I saw you, you were crying when your expensive shuttlecock got stuck in the trees, right?" I laughed.

"Hahaha, I remember that! I also remember how badly Dad scolded me then. But trust me, those days were golden. Nothing similar happened after we shifted to Saharanpur."

Saharanpur. The word alone brought back memories flooding that were locked up somewhere in my mind closet. Everything started on loop. **Saharanpur. Nani. Ankush. Betrayal.**

"Saharanpur?" I hesitated.

"Yes, we shifted there because of some family reasons. But now we are back in Delhi for my master's. I mean, we were anyway looking for reasons to settle back here, and see, I got one! By the way, why did you react weirdly to Saharanpur? Have you ever been there?" he said.

"My Naani lived there. She passed away two years back." Kartik expressed his concern and later invited me for coffee near the market. I didn't have much time to ponder my response, so I decided to go with the flow. I suggested he invite his cousin, Diya, as well, who used to be the senior member of our team during the games we played. However, Kartik didn't seem too interested and asked me again for the coffee. Meanwhile, we realized that for past so many years we were added on each other's snap time but never really interacted there. So he texted me with a 'hi' and that was how I got a new character added.

Upon returning home and facing my mom's complaints about coming home late every day, I attempted to take a nap but couldn't fall asleep. I started to wonder why Kartik wasn't keen on bringing Diya along, considering they were cousins. So, I decided to text him about it.

"Why not ask Diya to join us? After all, you two are cousins," I began the chat.

"She has her own stuff to deal with, I believe. If you ever get a chance to talk to her, you'll realize she's trapped herself in a complicated web of relationships,"

"Well, I shouldn't pry, but this sounds intriguing. What exactly is going on?"

"About an year ago, she started dating Devansh, her batch-mate. Their relationship was fine for a month, but then she lost interest. One day, she went to his home, and they had a physical encounter. There, she met Vivan, Devansh's twin brother, and that's when something clicked for her. Soon, she started getting attracted to Vivan. Things seemed okay, but she eventually and officially broke up with Devansh and started dating his brother. The interesting part is that neither of the brothers knows about her dual involvement."

"Oh my goodness! What a player! So, Vivan never told his brother about their relationship?"

"That's the problem. Initially, the two brothers were not on good terms, so Diya wasn't too concerned. She even had physical intimacy with one and then hung out with the other. However, their relationship has been improving lately; they even go to the same gym now. It is what it is. She's genuinely serious about Vivan, but if he ever finds out about her hidden affairs, he wouldn't hesitate to break up with her. And she can't imagine life without him."

"Therefore, serious relationships are injurious to health."

"Absolutely! It's become quite daring to dive into a serious relationship these days. Personally, I prefer socializing with new people, forming connections, enjoying some physical intimacy, and leaving it at that. Do you think that's asking for too much?"

Probably Kartik matched my energy,. He seemed intriguing and possibly my type as well. So, we made arrangements to meet up at a nearby café. I dressed in simple yellow top and black jeans and told my mom that I was going out with Diya to avoid too many questions, although she seemed suspicious, as I hadn't spent time with her in ages. We both lived in the same neighborhood and had gone our separate ways after college. I decided to leave as quickly as possible before Sneha could piece it all together.

Chapter 4

Hooked up? Seriously?

As I stepped into the café, my eyes quickly caught sight of Kartik waiting for me. Before I had a chance to greet him, my phone rang with a call from Abir.

"Ana, could you share a picture of the last page of your notebook that you brought today?" "Well, I'm out at a café right now. Why do you need it?" I replied, my tone tinged with confusion.

"Riva probably has called you there," he teased.

I explained to him that I wasn't out with her but rather spending time with a new friend. Abir casually accepted this and suggested I call him back whenever I get free. Just as I was about to end the call, I heard Kartik calling my name. We exchanged smiles, but I could sense a hint of suspicion in his gaze as he wondered who I had been talking to.

"Oh, I was just on a call with my best friend, he..." I began, but Kartik interrupted and cut me off.

"He? Your male best friend?" he inquired.

"Yes, he's been my best friend since high school, and fortunately, we're in the same college now," I replied with a smile.

Kartik chuckled and remarked, "You know, girls with guy best friends can be real red flags. Even if their boyfriends would move mountains for them, these girls might give those mountains to their best friends without hesitation. Initially, these best friends resist letting the girl enter a relationship, and even if by any chance she does, they'll still find ways to keep her close."

"That's quite unfair. Abir isn't like that at all, honestly." I said almost with that protective instinct in me. "In fact, he's gone to great lengths to make me happy. There have been countless times when he's comforted me after Sneha; I mean my mom's lectures. Whenever I used to feel down about not being able to learn to drive from my dad, he'd immediately take me out and reassure me that I could do it. Beyond that, he understands me better than I understand myself."

"Setting everything else aside, tell me, what have you done as a boyfriend in your life for someone? Then I'll tell you what my best friend has done for me in this lifetime. Trust me; it might make you reconsider your belief in committed relationships," I responded candidly.

Kartik remained silent, wearing a smile as he listened to my words. He admired how I stood up for Abir and was genuinely impressed by my loyalty to my friends. Little did he realize that it was likely Abir who had influenced my actions at that moment.

"As for your question about what I've done as a boyfriend," Kartik began, "I've left a trail of tears. I've been kind to a few and unkind to many. Some I've treated sweetly, while others I've left with bitterness. To a few, I've been a cherished memory, but for many, I've been a walking nightmare." He playfully winked.

I was quite impressed with his answer. He could see me being speechless and, therefore, ordered something to break the awkward silence between us. As the waiter came with two cups of coffee and a sandwich, I began asking Kartik about his master's to steer the conversation a little. He told me that he was looking for a distance learning degree and investing time in his dad's company. I was surprised when he told me that his father had to force him to join his well-running institute. He nodded and told me that he didn't feel like doing anything for days. I could sense the speech of a spoiled and privileged individual from his tone.

"If you don't mind, may I ask you something? Is he just your best friend, or is there something more than that?" Kartik hesitated, leaning in a bit closer.

"What if I told you I've never even held his hand? I don't have any romantic feelings for him. We share a deep emotional connection, that's all." I said with as much confidence as I could but still all of it felt bitter to my tongue.

He moved his chair closer to the table, locking his gaze with mine. "So, with whom do you share an intimate connection?" I chuckled to keep the mood in the lighter tone saying, "Certainly not with you, at least." He took it in stride, taking a sip of his coffee, "Intimate connections are important, aren't they?" he added.

I got a little taken aback with this abrupt shift in conversation.

"You don't need to be embarrassed about anything. We're adults, and we can have this conversation, if you're comfortable with it, of course," he added after seeing me get a little nervous.

"I'm not embarrassed; I'm just a bit taken aback because we've only just reconnected after all these years. So, I don't feel quite prepared for this conversation."

"I understand; please don't feel disappointed. I'd like you to be comfortable first. And for that, let's mutually decide to keep Diya out of this. Actually, I would prefer if nobody in the neighbourhood found out that we hung out together. Let's keep it private," Kartik's words began to perplex me. I couldn't quite decipher whether he was trying to make advances or if his words were just a means of evasion. So, I asked him bluntly.

"Hey, are you hitting on me by any chance?"

"Ahh, no-no," he replied, his tone assuring. "As I mentioned earlier, I see girls with male best friends as red flags. I genuinely admire the emotional connection you have with your... Abir. I was simply wondering if you were looking for a different kind of connection," he added, his hand lightly grazing his neck as he took a sip of coffee and looked at me.

"Isn't this moving quite quickly?" I was confused as hell. What on earth is he trying to imply right now? *Coming here was totally a mistake. A big mistake.*

"That's precisely what makes it easier, Ananya. Consider me proposing a committed relationship. It's a big decision, I understand that. You would discuss it with your friends, with Abir, and then you'd likely overthink past traumas we've all experienced. We will be spending several months getting to know each other, involving time, effort, and money, and what then? We might grow tired of each other's company, feeling bored, of course. One of us might even betray the other, and negativity would prevail," he explained.

"So, what are you suggesting, then?"

"So when you accidentally bumped into me today near the society entrance, I had this realization that there was something different I felt then. Our brief interactions of a few minutes truly left an imprint on me. I am not boyfriend material, I feel, but I've been thinking about the possibility of exploring a different kind of connection between us. I want to be clear that I have a lot of respect for you and our friendship, and I wouldn't want anything to change the dynamic we already have. However, what if we just allow ourselves to have a little intimate connection with each other till the time we are single, of course?"

Oh my God he is trying for friends with benefits situation.

"I hope you won't smash this hot coffee on my face, but all I am looking for is somebody who could match my vibe and considers this little intimacy to be normal and nothing more than that. No emotional strings attached." He added.

I took a moment to collect my thoughts, blushed slightly, and then nodded. He smiled, playfully asking if he wasn't too enticing for me to say yes. I responded by expressing concern that Abir might not be happy with my decision to start something this way. Kartik attempted to sway me further, suggesting that Abir was imposing restrictions on me, which was not the case.

"Life takes on a different flavour when you let your Id, the part of your mind focused on seeking pleasure and what you want, guide your decisions, rather than constantly abiding by the superego's ethical and moral compass," he delved into a psychological topic during our conversation.

His words convinced me to momentarily set aside the influence of the superego and instead, embrace the desires of the Id. He left me deep in thought. There was a certain charm about him that I had never encountered before. Moreover I have never been reckless in my life and my last relationship was a walking example of that. What harm it can cause? Above that, I also wanted a distraction the Abir chapter, distraction from constantly wondering upon him leaving for abroad.

"I believe I can give it a chance," I admitted, feeling a blush creep onto my cheeks.

Meanwhile, he received a call from Diya to whom he lied about his whereabouts. Afterward, he started inquiring about my relationship with Sneha and wondered why I had been calling her like that. I told him that I never had an immense connection with my mom and we were just two opposites sharing a roof. The only goal in her life was to see me getting successful and all my goals had everything other than settling down. I was meant to be chaotic and lazy at the same time. He tried suggesting ways to improve my relationship with her, but I knew that nothing could have brought us together.

Around 5 in the evening, we left the café and said a warm goodbye to each other.

"If you don't mind, I can drop you off if you're heading home," he offered, jingling his keys.

"Sure, that's not a problem," I replied.

With a friendly smile, he opened the car door for me. A street vendor approached us, eager to sell Kartik some flowers. I urged him to start driving and ignore the vendor, but he kindly reached for his wallet, paid a small amount, and handed me a yellow rose. His thoughtful gestures were truly capturing my heart. Maybe it is not a bad idea at all. I fastened my seatbelt, and we began our journey home.

Unexpectedly, he placed his hand on my right thigh, causing me to tremble. It was an entirely unexpected turn of events, and I was unsure how to react. He continued talking to me, which was a reassuring sign that he didn't want me to feel embarrassed. However, I wished I could convey that I was experiencing butterflies in my stomach.

"Ananya, please don't hesitate to let me know if you're not comfortable," he reassured me.

"I think we should take things slow," I replied with some hesitation.

He immediately withdrew his hand, and an awkward silence hung between us. To break the tension, he started playing music and asked me to turn up the volume. Things were getting back on track until we noticed a traffic police officer signaling us to pull over. Kartik made eye contact with me, urging me to sit upright and hold myself properly. He accelerated the car to its maximum speed, which left me quite frightened. It was undeniably adventurous, but it also had its scary moments. Eventually, he stopped the car in a dark spot and let out a sigh of relief. We exchanged glances and burst into laughter.

"Why did you do that?!"

"I don't like wasting time with this traffic police shit. And my dad is quite strict this way too. So I just escape from such blockages."

"By the way, in my presence, you're always safe." He added.

I chuckled and remarked, "I suppose you've flirted quite a bit with other girls too, and that's what's made you so spontaneous huh?"

"Huh, at least you liked my skills, right?"

I rolled my eyes and waved my hands in front of him and said, "Huh, it would be best if you could drive me back home. I believe we've ended up at completely different destinations."

He agreed with my decision, and just as he was about to start the car, he noticed that I hadn't fastened my seatbelt. Leaning in closer, he reached over to secure it for me. At that moment, I could feel his breath on my skin as he was remarkably close. Our eyes locked, and I gently rested my head on his shoulder and planted a kiss on his cheek. He responded by holding my hand and giving me a tender kiss on my forehead. I whispered, "Someone might be watching us." But he assured me that there was no one around. He then unfastened my seatbelt, and our kisses grew more passionate.

I ran my fingers through his hair, tilting his head slightly, and we shared a lingering, passionate kiss. His hands began to explore under my shirt, unbuttoning the top two buttons, and I felt his fingers tracing the edge of my bra. Just as things were heating up, my phone rang at full volume, displaying Abir's name and an 'urgent' text message and the spell broke.

"Babe, can't you ignore the phone call?" Kartik murmured, clearly hoping to continue where we left off.

"No, it's something urgent; I need to attend to it."

"What could be so urgent? Let's get back to what we were doing. Weren't you enjoying it?" he continued to kiss me passionately. I gently pushed him away and asked him to stop. While I answered Abir's call, Kartik's lips lingered, eager to continue.

"Long story short – Your mom is looking for you. Your phone shows unreachable. Where the fuck are you?"

"Abir, I'm with Kartik right now. We're on our way home. We had a run-in with a traffic police officer, and I honestly have no fucking idea where we are at the moment. Can you please ask Riva to handle it for me? Please?" The Impatient me.

"Relax. Send me your location on WhatsApp. Should I come to pick you up? Or is Kartik dropping you?"

"He is with me, and he's driving. We're just leaving," I replied, ending the call and urging Kartik to start driving. He seemed annoyed, not because I answered Abir's call but because I had interrupted our moment and pushed him a little.

"What's going on? I mean, I'm speechless right now. We need to talk about this, right here, right now." he insisted almost irritated with all the interruption.

"Are you out of your mind? My mom is trying to find out where I am. Even though I've messaged her that I'm on my way, she might be getting worried. Please, let's just head straight home. I don't even know where we are, and it's getting dark." I pleaded.

"See, I am not being rude to you but here is something I want you to pay attention on, babe. I am not your best friend who would handle these stupid dramas of yours; I have my own shit to deal with. I hope you understand that. Above that, I told you before, no emotional strings attached! So I think the next time this happens, you should..."

"Fine, I shouldn't have pushed you or expected you to understand my drama. Can we please just head back home now?" I interrupted.

Fifteen minutes later, I finally returned home, where I met with an inevitable lecture. I put the basket over Diya's head for my late return and omitted the part of my little expedition with Kartik obviously.

Would I keep resorting to escapism as my only response to my mom? Didn't I deserve to face it all someday? Perhaps she would comprehend, or maybe she wouldn't. Who could say for sure?

Chapter 5

'US' is what all i need.

After dinner, I retreated to my room and decided to study a little for my upcoming fifth-semester exams. Before beginning I changed into my night-time attire. Glancing at my phone, I noticed a notification from Kartik inquiring about if everything was safe at my place. When I answered him with a yes, he left me on seen, leaving me perplexed. I believed that he was pleasant throughout the day but he probably misassembled that I pushed him which might have him annoyed. Setting aside these thoughts, I decided to reach out to Riva and Abir before beginning to study. I told them bits and pieces of what all happened in the café and later.

"Well, I agree that his annoyance was right but he shouldn't have reacted like that. But honestly, it was just a fling. It's like, when you are in friends with benefits with someone; don't expect them to be good to you unless it's about being on the bed."

"Give him time. I guess whatever happened, it was really spontaneous. None of you had control then, so just RIC." Riva added.

"RIC?" I said.

"RELAX.IGNORE.CHILL."

Throughout our conference, Riva and I were the ones engaged in discussion and gossip, while Abir remained conspicuously silent. His silence was quite exasperating, as I wished he would communicate whether I was in the wrong or if something was bothering him. In the end, I interrupted Riva and asked Abir for his opinion. His response was unexpected and harsh.

"Why should I say anything, Ananya? If you've already made all the plans on your own, what's the point of discussing it now? Just a few weeks ago, it was Sameer you were involved with, and now this Kartik situation. What's going on with you? This doesn't seem like the Ananya I know. You shouldn't be getting involved in these chaotic situations, do you understand?"

Riva attempted to calm Abir down, saying, "Relax, it was just a fling. It's not like they are banging each of their heads out. Just a kiss. Big deal."

"You, please, stay out of this. You're part of the problem. You only misguided her." he retorted. "I've said it before, and I'm saying it again, Ananya, you're only creating trouble for yourself. We only have a week left before our fifth-semester exams, and college will be over in the next six months."

Tears welled up in my eyes, and I fell into an uncomfortable silence. Abir had never raised his voice at me like this before, and I found myself unable to justify his anger.

I knew I wasn't entirely right, but I was equally certain that he wasn't entirely right either. I tried to console myself, ended the call, and cried, clutching a pillow tightly to my side. I don't know what has gotten into me lately. With all this breakup and stepping into Riva's shoes plan is a feeling like I am hit with a storm and don't know how to come out of it. Abir is somehow right; sometimes I am also confused at my image in the mirror. This is not me. I don't do flings, I don't kiss random strangers, I don't follow the hook-up culture. *Oh god. What have I done?*

Within an hour, a notification appeared on my phone breaking me from the thoughts, and I initially thought it was a message from Abir. But a wave of excitement and confusion flowed through my veins when I saw the name.

Kartik:
"Trehan's concert at JLN Stadium this Sunday. You and me, in?"

I wasn't in the mood to make any plans with him. Instead, I remembered that this coming Sunday, Abir had plans to visit the 'Oberoi immigration office.' And obviously I would not have cancelled my plans with him because of Kartik.

Has it ever happened with you that the more you try to distract yourself, the more fucked up you end with the overwhelming thoughts? I tried hard pushing away the thought of Abir raising his voice at me but I had no energy to confront. Unconsciously, I knew I was at fault. Maybe that is what makes all of us resist confrontation, isn't it? I wanted to tell him how terrible I felt at that moment, how much I missed him, and how I wished to share my mixed emotions with him. His absence had suddenly become the most painful thing I was experiencing. Out of nowhere, I recalled a diary he had gifted me back when we were in 12th grade. I had always poured my feelings into it whenever we disagreed. The diary had its own beautiful story...

5th September,

It was our farewell day, and Abir had a strong desire for both of us to win the titles of Miss BNHS and Mr. BNHS at our school. However, I had opted to wear a suit instead of a saree, which made me ineligible for the competition. He was disappointed with my choice of attire and decided to play a prank on me by not speaking to me to gauge my reaction. Unfortunately, I couldn't hold back my tears, and by the end of the school day, I found myself crying. When Riva informed him that my tears were a result of how he was treating me, he quickly approached me and asked, "Were you seriously crying?"

"Yes, why does it even matter to you? You keep teasing me about my attire. I didn't want to ask Mom to tie a saree for me; you know that I had a terrible fight with her the day before yesterday, what do you expect then? And I am happy for you if you win the title! However, on top of everything, it's our farewell and just look at how you are turning a cold shoulder." I exclaimed whilst tears streaming down my eyes.

"Maafi milegi?" he chuckled while grazing his thumb on my cheek to erase my tears.

"I wasn't genuinely mad at you but I was just pulling your leg. Trust me; I had no intention of making you cry. Why on earth would I want to do that? I'd go to great lengths to protect my best friend from anyone who made her cry! Because..."

"Because?" I asked.

"Because you look really ugly when you cry!" he laughed and made me laugh as well.

"Shut up. By the way, what's that in your hand?" I pointed to the diary that he was holding.

"This is for you. I know we've made huge promises to each other to be there through thick and thin. I assure you of my emotional support until the end. However, in case I ever behave immaturely, like if we have a senseless argument and stop talking for a few days, I don't want you to struggle during my absence. This diary will serve as a means for you to jot down all your spontaneous thoughts. You don't need to worry about bottling things up. Think of this diary as a compact version of me, 'ABIR 2.0,' sound good?" He smiled.

"And I'll swap this diary with you whenever we decide to start talking again. Deal?" I said, tears welling up in my eyes. After the rush of emotions subsided, I began writing in the diary.

Abir,

I'm deeply disturbed because of you. Why did you react this way? You could have explained things to me; you could have listened to me. Instead of being gentle with me, you raised your voice, and I was already in a highly anxious state. For the first time in my life, you didn't do anything to help me out of a mess. I was casually discussing a day with you and you made me feel so embarrassed for what I did. I might tell to a lot of people that other's opinion doesn't matter but trust me, yours does. I wanted to hear from you. But all you made me hear was just silence and rudeness.

With that, I closed the diary and tried to get some sleep. However, by the time it was 2 AM, I started feeling a bit hungry, and my cravings for comfort food began to gnaw at me. So, I placed an order for a pizza and garlic bread. In about an hour, the delivery boy called me to pick up the order, and I secretly made my way down to the parking area to collect it.

But to my utter shock, it turned out to be Abir who was accompanying the delivery boy. I was left speechless and couldn't tear my eyes away from him.

"Ma'am, here's your order." the delivery boy interrupted our moment.

I took the pizza, but I couldn't recall the delivery guy's face at all because my attention was entirely fixed on Abir.

"What are you doing here?" I almost whispered.

"We both use the same account for ordering food, remember? I saw you had ordered a pizza, So I just came. By the way, may I come inside?"

"You're absolutely insane! If you were to eat pizza, you could have placed an order at your residence too."
"Oh so now you have a problem in sharing your food with me?"

"Huh! Keep quiet. Nobody must find out you're here under any circumstances. We can't go upstairs, and we have to be extremely discreet. Speak in a whisper, got it?" I cautioned him.

"What if I tell you that I'm also short on time, and I've paid extra to Anmol bhaiya to drop me here and pick me up in 15 minutes?"

"Who on earth is this Anmol bhaiya now?" I asked.

"He's the delivery guy who picked me up from my house and brought me here. There was no other option."

I couldn't contain my laughter, thoroughly amused by his ingenious plan. He gave me a knowing look and remarked, "It's all about the efforts."

As we shared smiles and laughter, Abir requested that I fetch the diary. He was quite confident that I had written something in it, of course he knows me so well dumbass, but I continued to insist that it wasn't a risk I could take at that moment and that I would send him a picture later. Afterward, I jokingly teased him about the pizza, telling him that he should feel honoured because I was willingly sharing my food with him.

"Ana, I really don't have much time right now," he began with a hint of urgency in his voice. "But I had to apologize for how I reacted. I've come to understand that what you needed from me was support, not criticism; my companionship, not my absence; my affirmation, not my resistance. I believe I've mishandled things between us."

I looked at him, a mix of emotions swirling inside me. "At least you came and apologized, and that means a lot to me. Honestly, I've been so self-absorbed that I didn't even text you once."

He interrupted, "But that's because you've been stressed and overwhelmed."

I couldn't help but chuckle. "How do you know me so well? You know, you're the exact reason I hesitate to get into a relationship. I doubt anyone in this world would understand me the way you do, and that's what makes me take a step back."

He teased, "Well, don't blame me, okay? So, how's your 'intimacy' with Kartik going?"

I laughed, a sense of relief washing over me. "Oh, don't make it a big deal! It's just a new phase, and I might put an end to it soon. It's simply because we shared a close friendship in our childhood; he holds a soft corner, that's all."

While we were talking, Anmol bhaiya texted him, reminding him to return home. As we were about to part ways, I wrapped my arms around Abir's neck in a warm embrace. It was as if that hug had the power to mend everything that had felt askew before. It made me ponder if a best friend's hug truly possessed such magical qualities or if Abir himself was just inherently special. It was like a blanket of comfort was wrapped upon me and no one could harm me here. *My safe haven.*

In the comfort of that embrace, I found solace and a renewed sense of connection. It was as if the unspoken words of our friendship had found expression in that single, heartfelt hug. He hugged me back and I felt as if he was also feeling everything different like me. There was this need in that hug that we both were craving, not just-friends hug but more-than-friends hug and none of us was ready to leave yet.

Chapter 6

I am proud of you, abir!

I was determined to resolve the tension between Riva and Abir and bring us all back on the same page. After a lengthy discussion, both of them apologized to each other for their childish behaviour. Meanwhile, I happened to glance at the notice board and saw an announcement for the portrait-making competition scheduled for the next day. I couldn't resist my excitement and wished Abir the best of luck, as I had confidence in his artistic abilities. Riva also joined in, and the three of us went to see Saloni Ma'am for more details.

"Abir, you need to be at the Art club tomorrow at 9 am sharp, and the competition will begin around 10. You'll have a maximum of 4 hours to complete your portrait and submit it to the designated teacher. By 6 p.m., you'll receive an email regarding whether you've been selected or not. The top 3 winners will earn a spot in the National Art Festival at Connaught place. There, you'll need to deliver a captivating speech, and the ultimate winner will receive a generous cash prize. But keep in mind that the art festival is scheduled for the coming Sunday. So plan your schedule accordingly." She explained with a smile and wished Abir good luck.

Naturally, he felt a bit nervous, knowing he had to face tough competition from other contestants. Riva and I did our best to boost his confidence and encourage him to give his all. I suggested him to leave college early to practice and refine his skills for the competition. Just before he was about to depart, he paused and whispered in my ear, "So, how's Kartik?"

I chuckled casually and advised him to focus more on his competition than my somewhat troublesome friend.

"On a more serious note, how's he doing? Did he reach out to you after that?" Abir began to ask after Riva left.

"Yeah, he checked in on me once, but honestly, I'm not jumping to any conclusions about him. I just don't feel like giving him too much importance right now. Undoubtedly, he's good-looking, smart, and intelligent, but maybe he's not my type? I mean, he's not a bad option for hanging out, at least." I chuckled.

The day passed, and finally, it was the portrait-making competition, which we had all been eagerly anticipating, arrived. Things went smoothly under the supervision of Saloni Ma'am and the other assigned teachers. We were asked to wait outside the Art club because only participants were allowed inside. I managed to sneak a peek through a small window and sent him my heartfelt wishes. *That's my passionate Abir right there.*

Within three hours, he approached us with excitement written all over his face, telling us about his portrait how he had crafted a magnificent idea depicting the destruction of wildlife due to human involvement. Filled with anticipation, we waited until 6 in the evening, when it was finally time to check the emails.

"Congratulations, Abir! You've been selected to represent us at the National Art Fest tomorrow. Please be prepared for your speech at 3:30 pm," the email read.

The three of us were overjoyed to hear this news, and we felt so happy for him, who was achieving something he had always dreamed of. He was a truly gifted artist, and finally, he was receiving recognition for his talent.

"Relax guys. I haven't won the competition yet. The speech round is still ahead. Ana, I'm counting on you. I trust you, and I believe nobody can craft my speech better than you. I'll call you tonight, explain my portrait, and you need to write the speech for me, okay?" he said with his eyes shining bright with belief in them on me.

He had that kind of unwavering faith in me like no one else ever had. He always believed that I possessed a magical touch with words and encouraged me constantly. His confidence in me was truly remarkable.

After returning home and having our meals, I called Abir that night, and we discussed his incredible portrait. It took me an hour to complete the speech, and he loved every part of it.

"So, you'll meet me tomorrow at the Pitampura metro station at 2:30 pm, and please be punctual. You know how important this event is to me, and I can't afford to miss it. I want to attend it with you, my talented writer," he said.

I assured him that I would be there on time and accompany him to the fest without fail. I slept around 3 a.m. yet managed to wake before the alarm rang. Then I saw a text from Kartik asking for the movie at 11:30 in the morning. I refused and told him that I had to reach at the metro station at 2:30 sharp. He tried convincing me that a movie would not extend my deadline, and that he would drop me before the time. told him that at any cost, I had to reach Pitampura metro station by 2:30 p.m. I hesitated saying a yes and he backed off. I kept my phone aside and went to freshen up. While I asked my mom to prepare the breakfast, my phone rang.

"Are you sure you don't want a movie day out?"
"I told you Kartik, I need to be with Abir for his competition. I have promised him. He would simply don't like me getting late."
"Who is asking you to break your promise anyway? I am just asking if you could accompany me for a few hours, the cinema is barely 15 minutes away from the metro station. Trust me; you need not to scare too much in life. Live it, take risks."
"Excuse me, I ain't scared."
"I don't think so! You are incompetent of taking risk. If I would have been at your place, trust me I would first enjoy the movie and then keep my promise to my best-friends. Things are simply easier if you don't complicate them." He said.
"Fine! At what time should I meet you at the cinema?"
"Umm, immediately after 30 minutes. See you there cutie."

I dressed up in a red tank top paired with blue denim along with baggy jeans to give it a little casual look. On reaching at the destination, I gradually untied my hair, wore the cute little scrunchie on my hand and there I saw him wearing red too. *What a coincidence!*

"I have already bought tickets for 'The Third Wheel' movie. Please walk fast now." He hurried.

"Wait, what? That's a three-hour movie, Kartik! It will end at 2:30 sharp, this means I won't be able to reach at the metro station on time." I was already panicking by the end of my sentence. I cannot, not even by a slightest chance can get late to Abir.

"Chill, I will drop you by my car. Don't panic. It's my responsibility to drop you on time." With this, he held my hand and walked straight to the movie hall.

As we were moving towards the PVR, there was a rush of thoughts inside me. I had never been on a movie date with anyone in my life. The only crazy theatre make-out stories I have heard were from Riva. And trust me, I used to find them really cringe. I mean, we blame babies and kids who create a nuisance in the theatre, why not these couples who really distract viewers like me. Huh. As Riva came to my mind, I thought of updating her about my whereabouts. So I texted her that I was going to watch a movie with Kartik. As expected, she texted back almost instantly and irritating me more with *my dumb decisions*.

"Oh my gosh. Didn't expect this speed from you huh."

"Shut up Riva. It's just a movie."

"NO. IT IS A MOVIE. IT'S A MOVE. DO YOU GET IT? (laughing emojis)"

I set my phone aside and began to gently ask Kartik whether we could exchange our movie tickets to avoid any time crunch. However, he grew agitated and asked me to remain calm and have faith in him. Unlike Abir, who had a soothing effect on me, Kartik seemed to be suppressing my mounting anxiety, potentially exacerbating the situation. How do I explain myself? I know I am a bit nervous but that's Abir, I want to be there for him and cannot disappoint him at any cost. Nobody or nothing is more important. *I repeat no one.* When

I responded with a grunt and started to ignore him, he promptly apologized for his mean reaction, realizing that it had upset me. And In an attempt to put me at ease, he asked me twice if I wanted to grab something to eat at the movie theatre, but I refused. *Kartik told me that irrespective of the time when the movie ends, we would leave the theatre early so that I won't get late. This finally brought me some calmness. But,* a text from Riva arrived that left me bewildered.

"Please don't inform Abir about this. He tends to make a big fuss."

I couldn't help but notice Kartik's growing unease as I continually checked my phone and glanced at the time. Frustrated, he suddenly took my phone and spoke softly, saying, "Babe, this is our moment. I understand your concern for your *best friends*, and I've already promised that you will be back by 2:30. What's bothering you?"

I nodded and took my phone back, though I was puzzled by my own reactions. Everything was proceeding perfectly. I had managed my time efficiently, and Kartik sat beside me – it was akin to my first movie date, going absolutely smoothly. Yet, an uneasy sensation churned in my stomach, and it wasn't the pleasant kind of excitement; it was guilt. The nagging thought persisted – was I doing something wrong? Was it acceptable to be on a movie date with Kartik without Abir's knowledge? Shouldn't best friends share these minor details, or was I merely overthinking it? I couldn't be sure.

"A penny for your thoughts?" Kartik peered into my eyes.

"Oh, no, it's getting too cold here, and I am seriously allergic to cold temperatures." I hesitated.

"You should close the buttons of your jacket for a while. I've known you since childhood; you've always been sensitive to the cold, and this theatre is exceptionally cold today." He thus put his hand forward and gently tied all the buttons of my denim. I didn't respond much; I simply wasn't in the mood to escalate things in the cinema that day. *My mind was wandering to brown eyes.* To be honest, the atmosphere didn't seem right. We were surrounded by a large crowd, and in front of us, a lively family with kids was causing quite a commotion. I took a deep breath and tried to focus on the movie.

"I don't mind if you rest your head on my shoulder," he was grinning like a love-sick puppy, making a subtle move.

"But I do."

"You're quite amusing. Anyway, it seems you're not comfortable here. I'm really sorry; I had no idea the theatre would be so crowded and this cold, with these obnoxious kids ruining our date. If you want, we can switch seats."

"Kartik, I think you're moving too quickly. Let's do this: watch the movie together, and we can talk about these things later."

"Come on, Ananya! Don't be so uptight. Is it too much to ask for a kiss?" He leaned in slightly, and I nodded.

"Listen, something has been bothering me. I don't know, but I just don't feel comfortable keeping this from Abir. I mean, it's just a movie date with you, but... I can't quite explain what's going on with me. And on top of that, this cold is really getting to me; I'm terribly allergic to cold weather. Nothing feels quite right except for the movie's storyline." I let out a sigh.

"So, would you mind if we watch the movie now?"

He replied, "I respect your consent.

"Even if you had simply said 'no' without any explanations, I would have respected it and backed off. So just relax and enjoy the movie."

I whispered an 'okay' in his ear, and we resumed watching the movie. We commented on the characters, laughed at the jokes, held each other's hands, and I was genuinely enjoying the moment. The intermission came around 12:30 PM, and that's when we went towards the PVR corridor and I felt a little relieved. While I was busy checking my phone, I caught Kartik staring at me with a cute smile.

"You know what? I find you rather perplexing. Sometimes you seem too good and other times, not so much. You can be dominant and submissive, easily annoyed, or incredibly chill. Are you intentionally juggling multiple personalities?" I asked.

"I dislike it when people accuse me of having multiple personalities, but I do have some anger issues. Once I get angry, I lose control, and that's probably why my past relationships failed. I was often the cause of it. I wasn't always the ideal partner. I had my own history back in Saharanpur when I was in the 11th grade. The best duo - Aarvi and Kartik. But my anger ruined it all."

Aarvi? Am I hearing right? Ankush again?

"Aarvi? Which school did you attend?" I asked.

"Kian International School. Why do you ask?"

"Well, I told you before right my Naani used to live there and she had a tenant named Aarvi." I tried making up with the situation.

"Okay, but still how does the school matter? Is there anything you are trying to hide?"

"My goodness, you think so much. I just tried knowing you, please relax."

"But I sensed something different when I mention ed Aarvi's name...I mean..."

"Kartik, please could you stop? I realy don't have the energy to extend this." I sighed.

I was left without words and overwhelmed with nostalgia at that moment. No matter whom you end up with in life, that first love will always hold a special and cherished place in your heart. But this time it wasn't the hurt surrounding my heart, just disappointment. I tried to pull myself back into the present as the movie began, and we continued watching.

As the movie concluded with a happy ending, and unexpectedly before the time, our so-called date came to an end as well. I couldn't help but smile, feeling proud of how smoothly everything had gone. The only thing currently exciting me was Abir's upcoming speech. I knew he had been nervous about it and had been practicing diligently. I sent him a message with an "I know you will do great" sticker and closed the chat.

"Would you like to grab a burger and a drink? We still have ten minutes until two," Kartik suggested, glancing at his watch.

"I think we should head back to the metro station. You'll also need to get your car from the parking lot."

"Relax, Ana. You seem to be stressing a lot. It will only take 10 minutes to eat and 5 minutes to leave. I know you're hungry too. Just give me a second I will straight away fetch something and we will eat it as soon as possible."

I ate hastily and urged him to do the same. I even offered him the option to stay at the mall and call his other friend while I left on my own, but he insisted on dropping me off. It took quite a while for us to finally get our car from the parking lot, and by then, it was getting very late. I was feeling anxious and worried, so I didn't dare to call Abir and update him on the situation. After taking an exit, we realized that it was raining heavily and we had only twenty minutes left to reach the metro station. Meanwhile, I received a text from Abir asking to be on time. I urged Kartik to speed up things and finally, he came up with the car.

As he realized how worried I was, he raised the volume of his songs so that I could distract myself from the intrusive thoughts of upsetting Abir by reaching out late. Fortunately, the car stopped exactly in front of the metro station sharp at 2:30 p.m. I felt relieved and texted Abir that I had reached. Before I stepped out of the car, Kartik interrupted,

"If he has not reached by now, you can wait here itself. It's quite cold outside and you already are sneezing a lot. Whenever he will come, you can see him quite easily."

His idea sounded impressive to me as I was already tired of walking in huge heels. Above that, Abir had texted me that he would be 10 minutes late so I started addressing the situation a little calmly and agreed to what Kartik suggested.

The atmosphere around us was painted in a wholesome dark, cloudy embrace, accompanied by the soft melodies playing in the background. My hands were cold and trembling, partly due to the chilly weather, and partly because of the tantalizing tension that had been building between us. Kartik decided to break the silence, unfastening his seat belt with a deliberate, seductive motion.

"Movie theatres may be cringe, but no one would decline the allure of sharing a moment in a car, right?" he teased, his words laced with a playful charm. His comment made me blush slightly, and I tried to divert my attention from the increasingly intimate situation. However, I found it nearly impossible to resist the magnetic pull when his fingertips gently traced my lower lip, slowly trailing to the left.

"What's holding you back?" he murmured, his voice laced with desire.

I hesitated, a mixture of excitement and restraint swirling within me. With a coy smile, I replied, "This car's seat belt."

He unfastened the belt for me, and that's when our date took an intense turn. Kartik's hands found their way to my waist, drawing me closer to him. I could hear his steady breath and feel his touch tracing a delicate path across my neck, then venturing further down to my chest. His touch carried an intense intimacy that overwhelmed my senses, making me lose control. I know you must be thinking that I should have resisted myself. But how on this earth could I express that Kartik was so good at this intimacy that the more I tried to resust him, the more his fingers, his eyes, his touch attracted me towards him. His touch was magical.

In response to the electric connection between us, I showered him with feather light kisses – on his cheeks and forehead, and finally, our lips met. The car became a realm where our desires flowed freely, in tune with the music that serenaded our passionate encounter. Kartik, driven by his desire, gently tugged my hair and caressed my face with his fingers, deepening our connection with every touch. As the song came to an end, a sudden realization washed over me. I swiftly checked my phone, and to my dismay, it read 3 o'clock.

"Oh my God. Fuck me. Fuck me."

"Only if you give the permission lol," He murmured.

"You think I'm just fooling around and joking? Why did we do this, Kartik? I mean, why?" I cried, my voice trembling with frustration and regret.

"I'm sorry; that was completely impulsive, and..." he began to apologize.

"You knew we were running late. You knew I hadn't told Abir about us, and still, you planned this whole thing. You're such an asshole."

"Are you out of your mind?" he shot back, his irritation evident. "Whatever happened was mutual, consensual, and perfectly normal. Do you have to create a scene everywhere? He's your best friend, you should be thinking about him. Stop blaming others when the real issue is you. You're the one who can't handle your relationships. I thought I was hanging out with a mature woman, but you turned out to be an immature idiot."

With intense panic mode turned on, I didn't engage in an argument. I simply got out of the car and searched for a place to sit. The strong wind blew dust around me, making it difficult to keep my eyes open. As the rain began to fall, it mixed with my tears, leaving me feeling exposed and vulnerable.

Amid my turmoil, I received a random call from Riva.

"I fucked it up, Riva! I am the troublemaker for real. I managed everything perfectly but somehow fucked it all at the end. I was making out with Kartik and just didn't realize when the time passed. What's worrying me more is the zero missed calls from Abir. How could he not call me?"

As I said this to her, I recalled Kartik's words when he told me that if in case Abir came that way, we would see him. I wondered if so he could have seen us together in the car too.

"No way! You are telling me that he had seen you fucking him?"

"We were just fooling around a little, or maybe more than a little, but trust me, his speech was my top priority! I don't think Abir saw us like that; otherwise, he would have called or sent a message."

"Ana, I think the last resort for you is going to his exhibition right away. Talk to him, convince him, and if necessary, apologize. I hate to say this, but you're in the wrong here. And yes, don't worry about your mom, I will handle her."

I couldn't stop sneezing and was overwhelmed by guilt for what I had done. I knew there was nothing I could do to ease my pain. I texted Abir twice, but there was no response from him. After the never ending and longest 30 minutes of my life, I finally arrived at the venue and searched for Abir everywhere.

The place had a lovely ambiance, providing a therapeutic backdrop with its beautiful paintings and art. After failing to locate him, I approached a random stranger to inquire if the speech round had concluded. They informed me that it had ended 20 minutes ago, and all the artists had gone for lunch together in the auditorium. I hurried towards the venue but was unable to get in due to strict rules imposed by the authorities.

"Please bhaiya, mera andar jaana bhot zaruri hai. Bas ek baar." (Please, I need to get inside, its really urgent.)

"Madam, gate 5 baje hi khulega. Uss se phele main kuch nahi kar sakta." (sorry ma'am, but the gates will open after 5 pm only. I am sorry, I am helpless.)

Upon hearing the disheartening words from the guard, I chose to wait for Abir. Riva suggested that I should head back home and address the situation later, however, I attempted to reassure myself that he hadn't witnessed my moment with Kartik and that I should stay there waiting for him. But deep down, I couldn't deceive myself. I could sense the truth, even in the absence of words exchanged between us.

"Madam, apko thand lag raha hai. Aap vapis chali jaye." (Mam you are feeling cold, please go home) The guard tried consoling me after seeing me shiver outside the auditorium.

"It is really important. Else, I would have gone back."

"Humare haath main hota toh apko zarur jaane dete." (If it were up to me, I would have surely let you go) He nodded.

I smiled and decided to wait till he stepped out. Finally, at 5, all the artists came but to my surprise, Abir wasn't there.

"Excuse me; I came here for Mr. Abir Malhotra? Has he left already?"

"Oh, Abir? He didn't come for the speech. God knows what happened to that boy. He was after me literally for today's event and he became absent."

Guilt punched me hard in the chest, emotions overwhelmed me, and I began to place the blame squarely on myself. The realization that he had missed such a crucial moment in his life because of me weighed heavily on me. I knew that I was the cause of his absence, and this thought consumed my every moment. I booked a cab to his home and told Riva to inform my mother that I was resting at her place and would be late due to the inclement weather.

I would have the courage to fight for you even during the toughest times knowing that you would stay by my side, but how could I get the courage to confront you when I have come to understand that I no longer have the right to ask you to be my side? Would you abandon me? Or stay?

Chapter 7

Turned upside down

Upon reaching Abir's apartment, I rang the bell thrice, and his mom answered the door. She noticed my pale and worried expression and inquired if I was okay. I simply nodded, and she kindly invited me inside. She offered me a glass of water and suggested that I take a moment to relax. Before I could say anything, she spoke up.

"I can tell you two have had a disagreement. Abir hasn't mentioned anything, but it's clear from his eyes. Should I call him here?"

Before I could respond, she continued.

"Or perhaps you could go to his room, and I'll bring some snacks for both of you."

With that, I made my way to his room, my hand hesitating on the doorknob. I had no idea how he would react, and the weight of guilt was overpowering my attempts at apology. Finally, I opened the door and found him lying on his bed, scrolling through Instagram.

"I'm sorry, Abir," I began, my voice quivering with regret. "I know I caused you to miss your speech, and that's the worst thing I've ever done to you. I'm truly sorry." He was lying there without acknowledging neither my presence nor my words.

" Please, say something, at least." I implored.

I was sneezing uncontrollably, tears streaming down my face. Abir didn't look at me once; he simply turned off the AC, knowing it was bothering me. In the meantime, his mom joined us.

"Ananya, the weather has turned really harsh now. You'd better stay here until the rain stops. And yes, you two can enjoy these snacks together," she said with a smile before leaving us alone.

I have to commend his mom for her understanding and maturity. She always allowed us the space to work things out together, rather than meddling in our conflicts. I took a seat in a chair near Abir's bed and suggested that we try to resolve our issues instead of ignoring each other for no apparent reason.

"Do you truly believe that my ignorance is without reason? Seriously?" He raised his voice sharply.

"I know, I didn't mean it that way. You have every right to your feelings. I realize how much this speech meant to you, and you missed it because of me. Trust me, I can't express how sorry I am, and I'm really disappointed in myself. You know me, and..."

"No, Ananya. I thought I knew you, but I was mistaken. If I had known that my best friend was involved with someone else in the middle of the road when she should have been at a crucial event in my life, I would never have called you my best friend. Is this how you treat your friends?"

I had no words to defend myself. It was evident that he had witnessed my actions in the car.

"All I'm asking for is one last chance to avoid any further chaos." I pleaded.

"Who am I to grant you a chance, anyway? Just a casual friend in a not-so-casual situation?" He responded with a dry chuckle without any humour, his tone filled with disappointment.

"Abir, you're completely off track here. Believe me, I regret what I did. I know it made you angry, disappointed, and upset, and those feelings are completely justified. But what happened between me and Kartik was just an impulsive mistake. I tried my best to be on time, and I actually succeeded! But you know how I tend to mess things up at the last moment. I know you don't really like Kartik, and I should have listened to you from the beginning." I tried to explain between sniffling and arranging my thoughts but everything seemed futile even to me. I shouldn't have gone to movie in the first place. Today was about my best friend, my Abir and I successfully ruined it for him.

"It's not about me liking or hating him; I can't quite explain it, but I just don't get the right vibe from that guy. Right from the start, I had this feeling that he would come between us and cause conflicts, and as you can see, I was right. I don't know if you'll believe me, but I genuinely know Kartik will harm you. Moreover, it's about me constantly sacrificing for you and your friends. Where do I fit into all of this?

"Listen, I feel a sense of insecurity when you're around these guys who, frankly, aren't on the same intellectual level as you. They seem oblivious to the fact that they're failing to recognize your true worth, treating you as anything less than a queen, and making you question your own value. It's painful for me to watch, especially knowing that you possess everything a man could ever desire. You're a complete package of love, a walking dream come true and it troubles me to the core to even think that you might offer it to someone who doesn't even deserve a fraction of what you offer. Ultimately, it will be you who gets hurt, and I simply can't bear to witness that."

I didn't even realise that I was holding my breath until this moment. His words are like a sharp pang to the heart. I try to calm my nerves and the sharp adrenaline running through my veins after his almost outburst of his calm and composure self. *Get a grip girl.*

"So, you're saying these guys don't deserve me or my love. Who does then?"

"I don't know. I can't stand seeing you get hurt because of anyone. In fact, I feel like punching myself for making you feel so bad about yourself." He broke down in tears.

"Why can't you see me like this?" I asked, my voice almost coming out in whispers and filled with longing for my best friend, who is breaking in front of my eyes.

"Because...I.." Abir keeps stammering and looks everywhere except me. After whole two-soul-shattering minutes of silence, I break it and ask in a firm voice,

"Because what Abir?"

"Because I love you damn it. Don't you get it that I love you? The entire class, the school, even Riva—actually, I think my mom also knows that I love you. But you, you've been clueless. The only person I have loved my whole life doesn't have a clue about it." he retorted.

"Ever since I shared my seat with you, I've been picturing sharing everything else with you. Like the last bite of my pizza? Or my favourite hoodie? Or my car, which I barely allow anyone to touch! But when it comes to you, I feel something different. Those fucking butterflies in the stomach, one touch from you and my whole body goes electrifying, that's how you've made me feel always.

"I hardly confessed my feelings because your story never had the space for me as the main character. It was either Ankush or these annoying little bastards. I was never a part of anything! I gave up on the idea of us dating after your first breakup. I wanted to give you space to process everything, not realizing that things would only get more complicated. On top of that, I had plans to apply for an MBA abroad, and Riva had already informed me about your status on long-distance relationships."

"Riva? She knew about it too?" I asked too dumbfounded after his confession. *He loves me? My best friend loves me? Abir loves me?* ABIR.LOVES.ME.

"She knew bits and pieces. She always insisted that you didn't have any feelings for me, and that was perfectly fine. I had no right to expect anything from you in return. But Kartik... he's someone I just can't stand."

"You said you loved me?" I interrupted.

"I said, I love you, and I always will." ---------------the huge silence prevailed. After gaining his sanity back he continues,

"Oh my goodness, did I just accidentally propose to you?"

I smiled, my heart pounding in my chest. Abir's confession hung in the air, filling the room with an unspoken promise. We sat in silence, each lost in our own thoughts, emotions swirling like a storm. And then a knock on the door and his mom's arrival with more food broke the spell. She scolded us for not starting the meal, and we began to enjoy the burgers. Between bites, I couldn't help but compliment his mom's cooking skills, grateful for the distraction it provided.

As we ate, I could feel his eyes on me, his emotions laid bare. The air was thick with unspoken words, and I finally found the courage to speak.

"Abir, I... I don't know what to say," I began, my voice shaky. "I never realized... I mean, I've always cherished our friendship, but I never imagined..."

He smiled warmly, reaching out to take my hand. "Relax; you don't have to say anything right now. Sometimes, it's just about the other person knowing how you feel. Even if that feeling comes with no response, it feels good to at least pour those things out that I just did."

We continued to eat, the atmosphere between us a mixture of tension and anticipation. Finally, I spoke again, "When are you planning to leave?"

He sighed softly, his gaze turning thoughtful. "After this week, we'll be done with our fifth-semester exams. Then I have my IELTS exams. In another five or six months, college will end, and I'll immediately move to Canada."

I nodded, absorbing the reality of his plans. The weight of his impending departure was like a punch to the gut, a reminder of the changes that would soon come to our lives. Despite the uncertainty, there was a sense of resolve in his words, and I knew that he was determined to chase his dreams. Infact I can never be a road block for him and i have always wished the world for him.

"Well," I said, offering a small smile, "I hope you excel in your exams, Abir. Canada will be lucky to have you."

"Thank you, Ana. Let's see where fate takes us."

Soon, we finished our meals, and I reluctantly decided it was time to leave. "I should probably head out now. The weather seems to have cleared up."

He walked me to the door, and as I stood on his doorstep, I turned to him. "Thank you for everything. I still feel miserable that you missed the speech because of me, but trust me, I would not let you miss this dream of going abroad at any cost. I would pray each day for you to reach heights!"

He placed a reassuring hand on my shoulder and offered a gentle smile. "Ana, you didn't make me miss anything. It was my choice to prioritize us, our friendship, and I don't regret it for a second. Canada still holds 6 months, so just stay calm."

I smiled back, touched by his unwavering support. With a final wave, I stepped out into the night, knowing that our bond was stronger than ever, even as our paths were filled with uncertainty. Regardless of the decisions we would make, I realized that our friendship was above all else. As I left his apartment, my mind was racing with a whirlwind of emotions. The day had finally ended on a positive note, but the butterflies he had given me were still fluttering in my stomach, a reminder of the complexity of our relationship. *Where do we stand now? He loves me, but do I love him? Does he love me like a friend? Does he think about me more than a friend?*

Four Weeks Later

Exams finally came to an end, and we were thrilled to make plans again. Fortunately, Abir had cleared the IELTS exams, and his preparations for studying abroad were in full swing. He left no stone unturned, trying for scholarships, collecting letters of recommendation from teachers, and seeking advice from seniors about settling abroad. Even when we hung out, he remained busy on calls with the Oberoi Immigration office.

Kartik had been removed from my life, and I had made a promise to myself that I wouldn't reopen that chapter. But wait; *are all promises worth keeping?*

What happened between Abir and me left a major impact on the bond that I shared with Kartik. After I realized his feelings for me, my heart no longer craved physical intimacy from anybody. In fact, I had never really craved that, it was just my mind drifting to idiot means of coping mechanism for my breakup. Abir was right from the beginning about it but I ignored all if it and here I am now, I found myself preoccupied with thoughts of what would happen when Abir leaves, and how will I manage to protect my heart to break for real this time. I can't imagine my life without him, without his support, without out late night ventures, without him forcing me to write, without him I am nothing. He is like the air I need to breathe and deep down in my heart I know that I cannot have him. *I am too late to love him.*

"My prayers must have appeared confusing to the Almighty. I found myself simultaneously yearning for his success and wishing for him to remain a permanent part of my life. However, I knew it in my gut that these two desires could never seamlessly coexist."

Chapter 8

Half semester only/-

Who claims that breakups inflict the most pain? The real anguish sets in when you realize you're about to embark on your final semester at college, where you've experienced the pinnacle of joy in your life. We could sense the conclusion drawing near, and the awareness that this marked the commencement of the end of my college adventure was a blend of excitement and nostalgia. As per our routine, the three of us made the mutual decision to attend college together, fully intending to skip a few course lectures.

Before Abir arrived, I decided to confront my best friend Riva, *soon to be ex-befriend.*

"You were aware that Abir had feelings for me right from the very beginning, weren't you?"

"I won't be a gatekeeper here, but yes, I had a strong suspicion that he harboured something for you. However, I couldn't help but question the point of pushing this confession further, especially when he was planning to leave for abroad in just six months. I feared it might turn into a replay of Ankush's situation. What do you think about all this?"

Honestly, I had no answer to her question, but one thing was certain - Abir's impending departure for overseas. He had always been the most career-oriented among the three of us, and his talent was truly exceptional. It was evident that he could build a successful life in Canada.

However, how could I allow myself to entertain thoughts of a future without him when I knew he wasn't just a chapter I could simply close, but a complete story I never wanted to end? Hello stupid heart, help me out here.

"Hey guys! I met Saloni ma'am on the way, and she was really upset with me for missing the event and disappointing her. I assured her that Ana would do it at my place. Now she has higher hopes for you for the anthology competition. Okay?" Abir jumped into the conversation.

"So, you basically brush it all aside onto me, right? How do I explain to you that I could barely write anything, and to add a cherry on the top, you are expecting me to publish an anthology? A book of poems? That is too much for me." I laughed.

Meanwhile, he tried snatching my phone and insisted I open the recent note in my folder.

"In destiny's hands, she placed her trust with care,
Believed he'd stand by her, through joys and despair.
Took him for granted, thought, 'Where would he roam?'
Yet the notion of his departure haunted her home.
Rarely did she express the feelings she held dear,
Gratitude is unspoken, emotions are never made clear.
Assumed he'd stay forever, a shadow in her stead,
But in time, she learned even shadows must spread.

For one day she grasped, in a moment of grace,
That even shadows, with time, find another place.
A lesson in love, a reminder, bittersweet,
That cherished bonds, in the end, may choose to retreat."

"Abir, stop it! I wrote this without any purpose. Its gibberish and no one can make sense of it. Please don't test my patience right now; the heat is already getting to me, and I..."

"Both of you, just be quiet! How about going ice skating today? You mentioned the weather, and it sparked an idea. I'll need to check if the tickets are available because the slots are almost full." Riva interjected.

"Count me in. I've wanted to go there for ages, but you guys were never available," he said with enthusiasm of a five year old who is just informed that he is going to meet DORAEMON. Later, we discovered that few tickets were left to be sold out, and we pre-booked a slot for the three of us in the afternoon.

As the three of us marked our journey, Riva and I couldn't help but notice Abir's constant phone calls and growing frustration as universities vied for his attention. I asked if he had decided where he wanted to enroll, and he promptly shared a meticulously planned list of steps he intended to take over the next five months to secure admission to his dream college. Unlike my somewhat disorganized self, he always placed his career as a top priority.

"The next station is Rithala." announced the metro.

With that, we exited, hailed an auto-rickshaw, and finally arrived at our destination – Ski-way! We suited up in the appropriate attire, each of us receiving long boots with sharp heels, warm coats, and a pair of socks. I struggled to tie the shoelace on one of my boots, prompting Abir to bend down and assist me with the chivalry of a true gentleman. My cheeks flushed with embarrassment, turned red like a tomato, and Riva captured the adorable moment. However, before we could revel in it, a passing couple remarked, "Goals, huh?"

"They're just best friends, nothing more." Riva chuckled.

The stranger guy retorted, "Every relationship starts this way, babe," glancing at his girlfriend. Riva's interjection bothered me, and when I mentioned it, she teased me about how I seemed eager for people to link Abir and me romantically. I couldn't deny the tingling sensation of warmth that washed over me when others admired us as a couple. Since our school days, people have labelled our unique bond as friends. But, the thought of being more than just friends sent a thrilling shiver down my spine.

"Let's head inside, girls!" Abir sounded genuinely excited. The place was freezing, with a temperature of -5 degrees Celsius, giving me goose bumps despite wearing a warm coat.

"I was considering asking you to join me for college in Canada, but seeing how you tremble in this cold, I wonder if you'd survive over there." he teased with a smile.

"First of all, Canada wouldn't invite an average academic student like me, and even if it did, my family can't afford it. Sneha is pushing me to start doing internships this semester. I've managed to keep her on hold for now." I laughed.

"It's high time you stop calling her that way. Respectfully address her as your mom; it's the least you can do." *Always the good sweet Abir.*

As we chatted, Riva joined us and reminded us to start ice skating, since we only had an hour inside. She began teaching us how to skate without falling too hard, although she had tumbled herself a few times during the process. I clung to the sidebars and sought guidance from an instructor. Gradually, I began to grasp the art of skating. However, I accidentally bumped into a large individual, resulting in a rather dramatic fall.

Riva and Abir rushed over to help me up, their laughter echoing around us.

"In a way, both of you have fallen," Riva quipped. "Excuse me, miss. She fell ON THE FLOOR, and I've been doing well for a good fifteen minutes." "I meant she fell on the floor and you... Well, in love..." She winked mischievously before leaving us alone.

She had created an awkward situation, and neither of us knew quite how to react. Finally, I broke the silence, "I wanted to talk to you about what happened between us before the exams. I appreciate your confession, but..."

"Look, you don't owe me any explanations. I know you've been overthinking it, and the stress is evident on your face. I know your answer, and I'm okay with it. Let's just forget what happened that day." he said.

"And what is my answer, exactly?"

"NO, with logical explanations, of course." "Why didn't you hope for a 'yes,' by the way? You're not that bad, huh?" I teased, winking.

"Haan toh ussi waqt ho jata hai, waqt toh NAA leta hai."

[Well, yes just happens in the moment; it is no that waits.]

We persisted in our diligent practice, determined to master the art of ice skating, and before long, I found myself becoming quite proficient. Amid our skating adventures, we found a mini canteen nearby offering steaming hot coffee, delicious Maggi noodles, and mouth-watering burgers on its menu. Riva ordered a combined meal for the three of us, and we sat down to enjoy a satisfying meal that warmed our bellies.

Just as she was about to place the order for Maggie noodles, Abir interrupted her, saying, "Make it less spicy, fewer veggies, and more corn, please. And a hot cappuccino with less sugar."

"I saved your energy Lol."

"I wonder if my boyfriend would ever know such details about me the way you do. I mean, I never knew that you remember exactly in words how I want my meal to be customized!" my words were out of my mouth before I could take them back. *Stupid, stupid brain.*

With about 10 minutes to an hour left in our skating session, we were beginning to feel a sense of boredom creeping in as the repetition of the activity grew tiresome. Our bodies were weary from the exertion, and collectively, we decided it was time to conclude our venture. We made our way back home, cherishing the memories of our ice-skating adventure.

Upon returning home, I was met with an onslaught from my mom. She was clearly upset. *Fun times.* "Neither you nor Riva picked up my calls, so I called Eesha, she told me you weren't in college. I understand you're making it a habit to squander your dad's money and have fun with your so-called friends, but that doesn't give you the right to ignore my calls, especially when it is something urgent."

"What urgency could there possibly be? Another round of career advice or more reasons to criticize me for enjoying my last semester with friends? Please, Mom, this is my final semester, and I want to make the most of it," I replied almost snapping at her. I am tired of all this drama of her all the time. Why can't she let me be? *I wish I had a mother like Abir's.*

"As if you were on your deathbed until now?" I believe Riva is the one putting these ideas in your head. She seems to control your thoughts, and you allow her to do so."

Of course she believes I am a gullible idiot. I grew increasingly annoyed as my mom unnecessarily dragged Riva into the conversation. I had begged her countless times to have discussions just between the two of us, but she always insisted on involving more characters. Managing to extricate myself from the conversation, I headed back to my room.

Before I could enter my room, I overheard her saying, "Tomorrow, your dad's friend, who runs an institute near CP, will be visiting. He's looking to hire interns, and I've decided to talk to him about you. Please behave appropriately."

"Which uncle? Why haven't I heard about any friend like this?" I yelled, bewildered.

"You were quite young when Kartik, Uncle's son, used to play with you in the neighbourhood. They moved to Saharanpur, but they've recently relocated here, and your dad has invited them over for dinner tomorrow. If he mentions a job or internship, don't you dare say no! We know you're uncertain about your future, so let us make this decision for you."

For a moment, it felt like everything was against me, as if life was about to force me to revisit a previous chapter I wasn't prepared to relive. I tried to explain things to my mom, but deep down, I knew it was futile. My family was adamant that I should start working right after completing my bachelor's degree. When I mentioned that I still had five months left in college, they questioned my ability to manage both academics and social outings. *I have to face Kartik again that too without creating any more fuss, already there spreading like a pest.* I was feeling trapped, *not to mention by my own parents,* I decided to call Riva and share some of the details of what a shit show my life has become lately.

"Listen, I know I might seem a bit confused right now, but honestly, I don't really understand Kartik. Sometimes, he's incredibly nice, as sweet as sugar. Other times, he gives me this vibe like he's a serial killer. Just try to normalize things with him, forget about it, and move on." she suggested.

"Right, there's really nothing to move on from. It was just a fling, you know that. The only thing that bothers me is that I made out with him, causing Abir to miss his event. And not to mention, Kartik has some connections with Aarvi, and who knows probably with Ankush too. I can't open two chapters at once for God's sake."

After trying to console myself, my main concern was Abir's opinion. He simply wanted me to stay away from Kartik, but destiny seemed determined to make me cross paths with him and put me at odds with Abir, for reasons I couldn't comprehend. I decided to first resolve things with Kartik and then surprise Abir with my thoughtful decisions.

It's a wonderful feeling when love thrives within your friendships, but it becomes disheartening and dispiriting when love starts to overshadow everything in the relationship. The connection that Abir and I had transcended labels, in my eyes. We were so deeply connected that no label could define us better than best friends. The mere thought of losing him was unbearable. He remained by my side when no one else did, even during moments when I had all but given up. He patiently waited for me to find my strength and stand tall, a constant source of support and unwavering friendship.

Chapter 9

Dreadful dinner.

In the morning, heavy rain poured down, and Abir informed us that he wouldn't be attending college due to a meeting related to his immigration plans. Riva and I hesitated about whether to venture out in such rainy weather, considering that classes were likely to be cancelled. Ultimately, we decided to skip college. So, my Wednesday unfolded like a lazy Sunday morning with nothing special on the agenda.

To add a touch of excitement, my dad decided to prepare (fritters) for the three of us. He was a skilled chef, and I always enjoyed cooking with him more than with my mom. It felt like I could share my personal thoughts with him, and he would wholeheartedly understand. However, Dad's demanding 9-5 job left him with limited time for us. As I assisted him in preparing the batter, he looked at me with hopeful eyes and said, "Ana, I know you don't appreciate how Sneha constantly pressures you to study, but as parents, we only want our children to succeed. We're not your adversaries. The reason I'm calling Sushant tonight is because I believe he can provide you with a great opportunity. You're talented and brilliant, my child."

"If only Mom conveyed these sentiments to me in the same way, I would never argue with her. But what can I do? I'm willing to give it a try. However, why only Uncle Sushant? I can figure things out on my own. Can't you at least give me a chance?" I pleaded.

I realized that my dad's stance was justified. All they had witnessed from me until the age of twenty-two was essentially me wasting time and enjoying myself with friends. It was high time for them, and they could no longer rely on me alone. Moreover, Uncle Sushant was a close friend of my dad, and he trusted that I would be safe and comfortable in that environment. My last—*only*--resort was to agree with him. Later, I discussed the same with Riva, and she understood that it was an appropriate decision to think of an internship during the last semester.

Within an hour, the rain began to ease, and I decided to head to a nearby grocery store for some essentials. As I browsed the store, I unexpectedly spotted Diya, who seemed preoccupied with selecting eggs. She had no inkling about the recent events involving her brother, Kartik, but for some reason, I found it awkward to make eye contact with her. I questioned myself, wondering why I felt so apprehensive about facing her. Before I could change my path, she called out to me with a warm smile. *Just my life, ha ha.*

"Hi Ana, where have you been lately? I hardly see you in the neighbourhood." she greeted.

"I'm doing well, just caught up with a hectic college schedule."
"I understand. Even Kartik, my cousin, seems swamped with his master's program." she commented.

"Oh, I should probably get going. My mom must be waiting for me." I hesitated and quickly made my exit.

As I walked away, I couldn't help but wonder why she mentioned Kartik's name. Was she trying to drop hints that she knew something about us? Diya was known as the unofficial news reporter of the neighbourhood, and the last thing I wanted was my parents getting wind of our history. To quell my anxious thoughts, I decided to follow Riva's advice and focus on the "RIC" principle. [Relax, ignore, and chill] After grabbing the groceries I needed, I tried calling Abir multiple times, but he declined my calls each time, texting me that he was in a meeting with a senior. He was understandably on edge, as his IELTS results could be released at any moment.

Upon returning home, I received an unexpected text from Kartik, which read,

"What were you discussing with Diya?"

"Why don't *you* tell me what you mentioned about me to her?"

"Ana, stop being suspicious all the time. Why would I do that? I've already apologized for what happened between us, but why am I the only one facing repercussions for it? You missed your friend's speech, so why am I dragged into this mess?"

"You have no idea how much you made me hurt that day. Still, it was me who sent you an apology text, but you just ignored it anyway, and now you seem to gossip with my cousin. Are you crazy for real? Dad is insisting me to come to your place and now I don't even feel like facing you!"

At least, we agree somewhere. I found solace in the fact that our mutual hatred had reached a point of equilibrium.

Though I couldn't rationalize his disappointment, it became abundantly clear that he would definitely oppose his father's offer of an internship to me, given the deep-seated resentment he harboured. Before I could unravel this intricate web of emotions, my father entered my room, wearing a warm smile, and gently urged me to research a bit about Uncle Sushant's institution – *"Will & Way."*

Will&Way was renowned for its excellence in digital marketing, MBA programs, robotics education, and media advertising. With three thriving branches in Delhi, its reputation was impeccable. As my father and I delved into their website, I couldn't help but notice a few errors in their content that immediately captivated my attention. In the midst of my scrutiny, my mother chimed in, her voice tinged with amusement, "Do you really believe you're more intelligent than the creators of this content, Ana?" She chuckled. Not a shock that my own mother doesn't believe in me. *But Abir does.* Ya right, Abir.

I couldn't think of a good comeback, so I just closed my laptop and lay down on the bed. My father lovingly stroked my hair, reassuring me to stop fretting and take a nap. Unfortunately, my nap extended longer than intended, and I awoke in the evening to discover eight missed calls from Abir. I knew instantly that it had to be about his exam results. My intuition was correct; Abir had aced the IELTS exam with an impressive score of 8 bands, and his joy was palpable.

"You know, Ana, Mom will be over the moon when she hears this news!", his overjoyed voice in my ears was like a balm on the wounds. I was so happy for him that I almost forgot about my catastrophe life.

"Haven't you told her yet?" I asked.

"No, you're the first person I called. I'll share the news with everyone later. I've been itching to tell you for hours, but you weren't answering your phone. I figured you must have fallen asleep during your nap."

Oh my god. My ovaries are not going to survive this. How can he be such a darling? *Abir is leaving.* My over-smart brain reminded me. *Listen this, you traitorous heart, shut up.*

"Canada is fortunate to have someone as foolish as you." I replied with a smile.

"But does that mean I'm an unfortunate smart guy leaving India, as you imply?" he pondered.

A moment of contemplative silence enveloped our conversation before I ended the call. While I was elated at his impressive exam results, I couldn't help but wonder why fate seemed intent on pushing me closer to Kartik while keeping Abir at arm's length.

As the clock struck 8 in the evening, we readied ourselves to welcome our guests.

The elders exchanged warm greetings, accompanied by endearing gestures, as they introduced Kartik and me to each other. Little did they know that their children had shared a stormy encounter just a few days prior? *Yes, we were wildly making out, but hello kartik. Not at all, nice to meet you.* We mustered forced smiles, fully aware of the underlying awkwardness and mutual animosity.

"I apologize for Kartik's mom not being able to join us; she's away in Mumbai for business matters. Speaking of business, Ananya, if I recall correctly, you were pursuing a bachelor's degree in *business and management*, correct?" he inquired, offering a smile in my direction.

"Yes, indeed. She'll certainly bring her mark sheet very soon. She's quite eager." my overly enthusiastic mother chimed in. We all took our seats, and I excused myself to the kitchen to attend to some preparations. I started to make lemonade for everyone while trying to find out the snack tray to be served along with it.

"I thought you might need some assistance." Kartik quipped as he entered the kitchen.

I chose to ignore his comment and focused on my task at hand.

"I'm sure there will come a day when you'll need my help." he remarked.

I couldn't help but retort, "Who invited you in here, anyway?"

"Your mom suggested it would be great if we could become friends. She believes it would help you feel more comfortable around our company." he explained.

"I clearly remember you were never really interested in your dad's institute. Why this sudden change?" I countered.

"So now you're going to dictate what I should and shouldn't be interested in? And, speaking of interests, I had no interest in coming here, it was my dad who forced me. But I think, we are on the same page. Neither you want to face me nor I. But I can't tolerate this attitude of yours. This is eating me alive."

"This isn't the right place for this conversation!" I snapped. "Please, for God's sake, just stay out of my life. If you despise me so much, there's nothing I can do about it. Just convince your dad not to offer me a job, or internship and it'll be that simple."

With that, I left the kitchen and decided to join the elders for a while. We were having a pleasant time until my mom started discussing my career with Kartik's dad. I began to resent her even more because she seemed to worry excessively about my future, and that overbearing concern stifled my ability to think for myself. Unfortunately, I was one of those children who were smothered by their parents' relentless concerns. *Fuck my life.*

"I suggest Ana starts as an intern in the media advertising department." Uncle proposed. "She can work with the sales team and handle promotions alongside it. Kartik can guide her since he has experience in this domain. But it will be a commission-based job. Once she graduates, I'd be willing to offer her a decent package of around 2 lacs but for that, she needs to dedicate herself fully to these five months."

"What about my college?" I asked.

"Well, we have plenty of undergraduates on board. If they can manage, so can you. If needed, you can join a bit later." Uncle replied.

"No-no, she'll manage it just fine. If others can do it, why can't she? I know Ana is very talented!" my mom.

Feeling overwhelmed, I sighed and retreated to the kitchen. Sneha followed me there and urged me to say yes to Uncle as soon as possible. I felt suffocated, as though there was no one to support me. I tried reaching out to Abir but he was preoccupied with his important shopping for abroad, so I called Riva and explained everything to her.

"Look, don't take this the wrong way, but you sound like one of those stereotypical girlfriends who's willing to sacrifice a great opportunity because of a guy who's about to leave for another country in a few months. You won't see him for years, okay? He's going to build his career, and you're ready to jeopardize yours. What's the logic in that? Just say yes, take the job. If necessary, work with Kartik; what's the problem? Colleagues can dislike each other, but that doesn't mean they can't work together or stay at the same company," she advised.

Her words rang true, making far more sense than my own irrational thoughts. In fact, I struggled to rationalize why I felt hesitant about working with Kartik when I knew that Abir would also be leaving for another country in just a few months. *I am not even his girlfriend; we are not in a relationship. Period.* One part of me yearned to take the job and begin the journey of settling down, while another part of me pondered how Abir would react when he learned about all of this. Throughout our friendship, if there was ever a time he had cautioned me to stay away from a guy, it was always Kartik! And yet, here I am, in the midst of an unexpected turn of events.

"Ana, if you're considering starting the internship, could you kindly fill out this form?" Uncle suggested as he gestured for me to check my email. Before I could respond, Kartik interjected, offering to assist me in completing the form. I arched an eyebrow at him, and my mom proposed that we both work on it using my computer in the room. With this plan in motion, we proceeded inside, and Kartik began powering up the computer.

However, I pushed his hand aside and exclaimed, "What the heck is going on? I explicitly asked you to decline your father's offer, and now you're here helping me fill out this form. Yesterday, you were apologizing, and today, you're acting bossy. Are you out of your mind?"

Kartik responded, "I've changed my mind. Now I want you to work at my dad's institute. Plus, let's keep this attitude in check."

"By the way, I know you have some terrible connections with Saharanpur and I think Sneha would kill you for having such terrible remote past and wild recent memories. Don't you think so?" He added.

I got scared on hearing him mentioning about Saharanpur repeatedly. I know I was a mere teenager then but Sneha would never understand this. In fact, I imagined the worst consequences whenever it came to my mom and her ability to understand me. Though I pretended to act rough to Kartik's warning, deep down I was slightly scared. Because Kartik was indeed unpredictable.

Abir could have provided with a more logical solution but, I knew bothering him was out of the question, as he was busy with his immigration matters. I also felt guilty for keeping things from him. I finally requested Kartik to stay out of my life and leave. His father unexpectedly came in and intervened, saying, "Son, why don't you help your aunt in the kitchen?"

I was flabbergasted, unable to sit still for a moment. The persistent thought racing through my mind was that he must have overheard our conversations and might inform my parents about it. I couldn't muster the courage to look at him, so I kept my gaze fixed on the wall. His father, however, came and took a seat beside me. In a hushed tone, he began,

"Take a deep breath, Ana. Neither I am here to inquire about what happened between you two, nor am I interested in knowing anything that happened with you years back, and trust me, I will not discuss it with your parents. But there's something I need you to know. My son is grappling with a moderate level of *bipolar disorder*, where he switches his mood and personality from depressed to sometimes maniac along with anger issues, and has shown self-harm tendencies. His previous experiences with classmates in Saharanpur had a profound impact on him, prompting us to relocate for his well-being. Despite our best efforts, we've struggled to make his world a better place. We've enrolled him in a prestigious college, but he rarely attends. We even arranged for the best therapist, but Kartik sabotages the sessions by missing them, making excuses, or failing to trust the therapist. We've tried pampering him with materialistic comforts, hoping it would make him feel privileged and that his life was sorted, but nothing seems to work."

As I listened to Kartik's father, something weird crept into my system. He had a disorder, I had sensed something was amiss in his behaviour, but I never delved into it. I began to wonder if I bore some responsibility for his condition. My mind went blank, and I couldn't find the words to respond.

"It wouldn't be fair for me to expect you to solve his problems." Uncle continued. "But the least you could do is avoid making things worse for him. Can you promise me that, Ana?"

I simply nodded, and at that moment, my mom announced that dinner was ready. Kartik's father was about to leave the room but paused at the door, adding, "*And please, don't be afraid of him. A broken soul can't break another soul."* He smiled reassuringly.

"I'm sorry, Uncle," I finally broke the silence. "I've done nothing but just used him. I want to help him now. I'm willing to work with him. I know we've had a terrible past over the last two-three months, but today I realize that perhaps he wasn't fully aware of his actions. He needs to confront his feelings, and I'll do my best to help him out of this. I will co-operate with you."

"Dear, nobody has ever done anything for my son." Uncle sighed. "He cries every night, haunted by memories of his previous school. He swings between being overly emotional and sensitive on one hand and completely apathetic and aggressive on the other. I don't want him to keep running away; I want him to confront these challenges. Maybe you both working together can make a difference. Maybe you can convince him to take the therapy seriously."

"What happened in his past school?" I asked to which he had no response. Kartik kept it a secret from him I guessed.

After a beat of silence I said, "So, when can I start at your organization?" We continued with dinner, ending it with some delicious gulab jamuns. I noticed Kartik trembling at times, frequently visiting the restroom and rubbing his head incessantly. It was clear he was becoming anxious. So, I served him a glass of juice with a reassuring smile, and his father seemed to understand. I knew that my actions were driven by concern, but I couldn't help but wonder if Abir would understand or if I should keep this from him. The uncertainty weighed on my mind.

Chapter 10th:

Confusion, confusion everywhere. Not a single brain cell to think.

"I apologize, Ana. I shouldn't have spoken to you like that. Believe me; I never intended to be so harsh. Let's forget what happened," read Kartik's text. I asked him to calm down and informed my mom that I would be starting the internship next month. She was over the top hearing the news, and my dad also encouraged me to take this step. As I sorted things out at home, I anticipated that it would be challenging to navigate the situation at my college.

When I arrived late, I saw Abir and Riva attending class together. I waited for them to finish and mentally prepared myself to confide in Abir. But he beat me to it, before I could say something.

"Ana, I have some news! The college I applied to has accepted my letter. Now, I just need to submit my documents, pay the fees, and handle a few other details." he said. I plastered a smile on my face and said, "That's fantastic! I'm so proud of you, Abir! We should celebrate this news!"

Seeing how happy he was, I didn't want to spoil his moment. At that point, all that mattered to me was his happiness, and I decided not to risk complicating things for him. Riva suggested keeping things to me until Abir paid his college fees and settled in a bit.

The month passed, and I continued to hide the truth from him. He was still unaware of the dreadful dinner, Kartik's hurtful words, and, most importantly, my upcoming internship at his dad's institute. They say that to hide one lie, you have to tell a hundred more, and it felt true in my case. I simply didn't want to disrupt his happiness or create complications before he left.

Throughout the month, the three of us had a blast. We skipped lectures together, crashed a wedding, and explored some obscure, unheard-of places. One memorable adventure was our visit to Manju ka Tila, where we had amusing encounters with foreigners. Lastly, we spent a lot of hours at the college pool table. At the end of the month, Abir urgently requested a meeting near the Yoga complex. I figured that Riva would also join, but to my surprise, he had called me alone. As I left home for our meet-up, my mom's words echoed in my mind, reminding me to prepare for my upcoming internship starting the very next day. I assured myself to share the update with Abir today as I had already hidden the same from him for a month.

As we finally met, he dropped an update, his voice tinged with a mix of excitement and apprehension.

"Ana, it's all set. I'm moving to Canada in three months. Right after our last semester exams in the third month, I'll be catching a flight within two to three days. My brother settled there and has made all the arrangements. We've got these two months to make the most of our time together, then the exams, and after that..."

I instinctively hugged Abir, offering my heartfelt congratulations and I just want to be close to him. I could sense the weight of this significant decision on him, so I tried to uplift his spirits, assuring him that everything would fall into place. I reminded him of his exceptional skills and talents, believing that he was destined for great things.

"What's wrong? Why are you looking at me like that?" I asked as Abir continued to gaze at me, his eyes reflecting a whirlpool of emotions.

"I'm not afraid that I won't settle there. I'm more concerned about whether I'll unsettle everything between us. Have I made the right decision to leave everything behind and move to a new country? Will I be able to sustain myself, or us? You know how much you mean to me, and the thought of leaving you, leaving behind five years of memories, is haunting me. Don't you feel the same?"

"I'm even more afraid than you. No. I am terrified. The thought of losing you makes me feel vulnerable, but I know that memories stay with us even when people grow distant."

Hearing this, he hugged me tightly, his tears a testament to the depth of his emotions. It was the first time I had seen him rests his head on my shoulder and cry like this. Our stories were diverging onto different paths, but the pain of separation was the one thing we had in common. We didn't need words; that hug conveyed more than words ever could.

"I love you, Ana," he whispered. And I could feel my heartbeat clearly at 200 pulses per second. How do I say this?

Do I even feel the same? I don't know, I just can't imagine my life without him in it. I can't think of a time when he wasn't there with me, for me, holding me tight. Now, everything is slipping like sand from my fingers, just like whoosh. Was I scared to accept that there was something more than friendship between us?

"Love fades away, but what we share is more than love; it's a true friendship, isn't it?" I replied, gulping the lump in my throat, my voice tinged with hesitation. Time was slipping away, and today was the stark reminder of our remaining time. I had only two months left to spend with Abir. My closest confidant was going overseas, and the uncertainty of a world without him loomed ahead. He was not just my go-to person for everything; he was my anchor, my home. His presence filled all the colors of my life, and his absence was going to disturb me like nothing else in the world. That hug we shared was so overwhelming that it made me forget to tell him about the new internship at Kartik's office. Or did I not get the guts to face him with the reality?

Later, we bid each other a warm goodbye, our hearts heavy with the unspoken words. As I made my way back home, I called Riva. She immediately asked if I had been honest with Abir about the internship. I confessed that I couldn't bring myself to tell him, especially mentioning Kartik's name in front of him felt impossible.

"Why are you being so scared? He is not your boyfriend! He is just a friend, okay?" She reasoned.

"What we share is something more than friendship, and you know that as well," I said.

"No, wait. What you had with Kartik was more than friendship. How can you and Abir be more than friends?" she questioned.

"Look, 'more than just friends' is only about intimacy. Is this what you mean? No, I can't explain, but with Abir, things are different. I agree I don't love him the way he does, but I genuinely consider him as my best friend. That's why I have decided to quit this internship. I will see what happens, but I'm not hurting him anymore. That's final!"

"Are you serious? Your mom would spare no effort in lecturing you about your career. If there's ever been a time you've made her happy, it's because of this internship. And now you plan to disappoint her? And those crazy stupid ass promise to his dad? Listen, Abir despises Kartik because he thinks Kartik might someday disrupt the bond you guys share and would harm you, right? But do you really think that's possible? Kartik has no romantic feelings for you; he has his own life tangled. It is his condition that makes him little deviant from us, but he must be good as an individual, as mentioned by his father that he would never hurt you." Riva reasoned. "Just tell Abir you're doing an internship somewhere, and boom! No more cross-questions. And if by any chance things get worse, I'm here. I'll handle it for you, okay?"

With this, she assured me that she would ensure I didn't lose Abir, and he would remain unaware of the details of my work. Hoping for peaceful two months, I agreed to her plan, aiming to proceed smoothly.

As I arrived home, I noticed my mom diligently ironing my clothes and inquiring about my outfit choice for my first day at the internship. Dad chimed in, humorously remarking that

Mom seemed more excited than me about this new chapter in my life. I found myself caught in the middle of their excitement. Striving not to disappoint anyone in my life and ensure their happiness had become a weighty burden. Little did I know that this endeavour was causing me more sadness and disappointment? I managed a smile and retreated to my room. After freshening up, changing into my comfy pj and t-shirt, and putting on my ear buds, I found a moment of peace. It was therapeutic, allowing my thoughts to unravel. I attempted to take a nap, but my racing thoughts held me captive. They continued to chant same words, Abir, internship, Canada, I LOVE YOU. OH SHIT!!!

So, I called Riva, and the first question she fired at me was whether I loved Abir or not. I grappled with this, knowing it wasn't love because if it were, I'd be willing to let him go. But, all I truly wanted was for him to stay—selfish, wasn't it? How could I equate selfishness with love? Therefore, I probably loved him but I was not in love with him.

"Have you thought about what will happen after these two months? In the blink of an eye, he'll be gone. And me? Struggling to maintain a long-distance relationship, just like what I went through during Ankush's chapter? I am not prepared for that kind of turmoil again." I cried. "It's not that I don't like Abir. He has everything I could ask for. In fact, he knows me better than I know myself. From my food preferences to the outfit I detest the most, he knows it all. I still can't get over the day he came with Anmol bhaiya just to apologize and make me feel better. But I also remember the day he missed his important event just because of me."

Before I could hear what Riva had to say, Mom came in and served dinner right to my bed. When I asked her why she didn't call me out, she gently told me that she thought I was sleeping and didn't want to disturb me. Although I always wanted Sneha to be affectionate and caring towards me, I wanted to have a reason to quit the new beginning, but fate probably destined everything so well for me that even when I constantly prayed for things to get complicated between me and mom, she showered me with more love, making it difficult for me to change my decision.

I tried everything possible to ensure I didn't lose him inadvertently, but I still wasn't sure if my efforts were enough to keep him safe forever. A part of me wanted to bid him farewell and wish him all the success for his new journey, while another part of me fervently prayed for him to stay. Every day, I found myself torn between hoping for his departure and silently wishing for him to remain. I was just lost in this confusing duality.

Chapter 11

Corporate girlie tryna balance life with love.

By nine in the morning, I readied myself for my first day at the office. It marked a proud moment not just for me, but for my entire family. Riva sent her best wishes, reminding me to be patient with Kartik. *All the very reason I was here in the first place.* I acknowledged her advice and had breakfast with mom. Shortly after, Dad dropped me off in his car, encouraging me to work hard and never hesitate to voice any concerns. With a nod, I gave him a weak smile and headed into the office. *Shall I say my new office?*

The commute took about an hour, during which I realized that the office was conveniently located just 20 minutes away from my college. I realized that this proximity made it feasible to meet Abir and Riva in between if needed.

"Good morning, Uncle." I greeted Kartik's father as soon as I stepped into the office.

"Good morning, *beta.*"

"I've discussed with Miss Kanupriya, and she will provide you with comprehensive training today, spanning 3-4 hours. Feel free to approach me if you have any further doubts, okay?"

I nodded and asked hesitantly, "Will Kartik be coming today?"

"Ahmm, I don't think so. But you carry on with the work." he assured, providing a glimpse of the day ahead. I reminded myself not to dwell on it too much, attempting to shift my focus. But as I turned a corner, I found Kartik standing there, absentmindedly rubbing his hands together. *Talk of the devil.*

"I thought it was your first day; many people must have wished you luck. Let me be the one to ruin it." he teased, a mischievous smile on his face.

"Even to ruin it, you need to work with me. And I have my doubts if you know how to!" I retorted, trying to maintain a professional tone.

"Excuse me; our office in Saharanpur had excellent supervision from my end. In fact, even during my high school years, I was involved in some business projects with my dad. Things changed afterward, I agree, but you should never really doubt my skills." he said with a wink.

"I find that hard to believe. If you were that good, why did you leave it all behind? It seems like you don't visit here very often."

"Things don't remain the same always. I just don't feel like working anymore. We're all going to die eventually, so what's the point of working so hard?"

We were directed to a specific training room, where our real journey began, accompanied by ten other trainees eagerly awaiting our arrival.

"So, I am going to train you all on managing data in Excel sheets, utilizing the portal, and troubleshooting server errors. There will be a test afterward. Are you all ready?" the trainer announced.

Everyone nodded in agreement, and we delved into the lesson. Kartik's dad observed us from behind the doors, visibly pleased to see his son actively participating in the session. I received a *thank-you* text from Uncle, and in jest, I assured him that based on Kartik's enthusiasm in this training session, he might consider attending a therapy session soon.

The lecture was quite impressive and concluded around 2 p.m. Before the test, we were granted a 20-minute break to unwind. Heavy footsteps approached me and Kartik was there, standing behind me asking if I wanted to grab some coffee. *"He even gets triggered because of a damn coffee."* His father's earlier words rang in my ears so I politely declined his offer. As we chatted about the session, I suddenly started coughing and sneezing uncontrollably, causing him to become concerned.

"Don't worry; it's probably the AC. I think I'm becoming more allergic to the cold than I ever was. How am I going to survive this ahead?" I wondered aloud; my mind filled with apprehension.

"Relax, shall I order a hot tea from the canteen? Trust me, it will make you feel better." Kartik said.

"Thank you, sir, but I really don't drink tea!"

"So what? If it makes you feel better, you should definitely have one. I am ordering it." he insisted.

"Wait. If something makes us feel better, even if we don't like it, we should still have it anyway. Is that what you're trying to say?" I winked playfully.

"May I know where are you heading to? Don't play with me Ana, okay!"

He ordered me tea and we sat there talking. He expressed how his dad would be overjoyed to see him in the office for more than at least two hours. Curiosity got the better of me, and I hesitantly asked him why he never seemed to take his office or college seriously. To this, he had no concrete answer and seemed to be evading the conversation. I thought maybe I crossed the bridge too soon but after a long pause and a deep breath, he opened up and confessed, "I think I am a failure. Ever since I completed my high-school, I just feel like a burden on dad like I haven't done anything to make him proud and I am just a failure in my own eyes." The weight of unspoken pain was palpable in his words.

Sensing the depth of his struggle, I began to inquire a little more about it. However, as I probed deeper, he started to act increasingly frustrated, defensive about his past, and reluctant to share more. It was evident that whatever happened, it was profoundly sensitive and painful for him.

"Why are you prying into it? That's none of your business. It's my trauma, and I don't feel like sharing it with anyone. Just go." he yelled.

I felt a sharp sting of rejection flat on my face and feared that maybe whatever progress I made with him will be back to square one if I didn't stop right now. So, without letting anger consume me or shouting back, I grabbed my bag and left the canteen. Sometimes, it's better to ignore an undesired response than push too hard to inquire about it. Ignorance can indeed be bliss, and Kartik needed that. To make him realize the importance of opening up and respecting others' boundaries, I chose to remain silent and headed back to the training room where the other interns were taking their tests. As expected, he didn't show up and spent his time in the canteen instead.

After we got our test scores, I went back to check on him and I found him crying.

"Kartik? Are you fine?" I asked him after kneeling to his side.

His red swollen eyes came into view and he said, "Everything just reminds me of that lady. I cannot get myself rid of her thoughts."

"Is she trying to bother you again? If this is so, I will talk to her."

"Nobody can talk to her, she only haunts me and only I understand her language."

"Tell me more about her, where does she live? How does she communicate with you? Do you know somebody from her family?"

As I dropped so many questions to him, he felt a little nervous, and I could see his hands trembling and legs shaking. He told me that he would feel anxious if I would tell things to his father. I assured him that I wouldn't and that he could share anything with me. Even after assuring him multiple times, he didn't confess his past and rather tried diverting the conversation to the test scores. I respected that.

"I got an A, and you seriously missed the test? I thought you would give me tough competition, isn't it?" I teased.

"I know you're superb in literature; nobody can beat you in that. The test, anyway, was for your grammar and vocabulary check. I would have lost it, I know," he sighed.

I took a pen out of my bag and gently held his hand, writing an 'A+' on his palm and smiled. "Sometimes, life is all about believing in you. If you won't give a chance to conquer this smile, nobody else will." I said, trying to uplift his spirits.

He held my hand in a death grip like he was craving to hear this from someone and said, "Thank you so much, Ana. Never in my lifetime did I expect that a childhood friend of mine would come back into my life unexpectedly and treat me this way. You unknowingly have done a lot for me, and I could seriously never repay you for this, I am sorry I threatened you with your remote past, I think I owe you something good."

We returned to the working space of the office. His dad informed me that the training for the day was completed, and I could leave if I wanted. I texted Riva if she could meet me, but she was busy with her college dance society and so was Abir was with lectures. So, I decided to leave. Uncle suggested that Kartik could drop me off since it was my first day. Initially, I declined, not wanting to inconvenience him, but he still got there.

As we sat in the car, it felt nostalgic. Memories of our past interactions in this car months ago were still fresh in my mind, making me feel both thrilled and guilty.

"Who–would have thought that we will end up like this, isn't it?" he hesitated.

"Who–thought it would be so much fun to work with you as an intern, eh?" I smiled.

"I can give the fun the other way round too" he winked. "Hey, don't be serious, okay? I am just kidding. I am all clear with my intentions now. You are my good-friend!" he clarified.

"Thank you for the clarity, but... the only good friend I have is Abir. Nobody can replace him, okay?" I smiled.

"You know, when you left me in the canteen, I felt a strange mix of emotions. I needed a moment to process what had transpired - how I reacted, how you allowed me to make space for the same. I felt a maelstrom of thoughts and feelings. Then, the realization struck me. Missing the test, felt a little upsetting to me. How your friend must've felt about missing that speech, right? Who could have stepped in and given an A+ performance for him? I wonder."

"Ahmm, yes, he was indeed saddened by missing the speech, but I carried an even heavier burden of unhappiness and guilt. It was because of me that he missed his event. I know him well; he considers me very important. He's the kind of person who would, without second thoughts, let go of a remarkable opportunity just for me. Say, if I were to suggest him staying in Delhi, he might even forfeit the chance to go to Canada for his master's!" I sighed, weight of the situation sinking in.

"Well, is that the reason you're hesitating to start a relationship with him? Because you know that you will anyway get distant?" Kartik probed.

Am I so easy to read?

"Ugh, you think a lot."

"You forgot to mention, 'in the right direction?'" he teased, laughter bubbling between us.

Maybe, unknowingly, he had touched on the right nerve. Amidst our laughter, the blaring music, and our profound conversation, he made me realize once again, why I wasn't ready for a relationship just yet. I smiled, allowing the insight to settle within me, and carried on as usual. But soon, it was time for him to drop me off.

"Hope to see you tomorrow. Mr. enemy?" I said playfully while getting off his car.

"Friends leave, enemies, *stay*!" he grinned a playful edge to his words, leaving me with a smile on my face.

Upon returning home, my mom was eagerly waiting to hear about my first day at the office. I laughed and asked her if she ever showed this level of interest in my college life, perhaps our relationship wouldn't have been so strained. She retorted, mentioning that I never seemed appreciative of anything going well in my life and tended to voice complaints about everything. The argument escalated, and my mom's frustration with my perceived indiscipline came to the forefront.

"I was trying to have a decent conversation with you, but you always find fault. Grow up, Ana!" she exclaimed.

"All I said was that you never showed this much love and concern to know about my college or friends, and look at you now! Is it only my career that matters to you?" I retorted.

"I realize it's a waste of time talking to you. I am already running short on time, and I need to leave urgently for the kitty party. Take care of the house. Do not make it a mess. Dad will pick me up around 9 or 10 at night. I've already prepared your meals; just use the microwave and get it. Bye."

With that, she left, and I took a deep breath, realizing that it had been a long time since I was alone in my own home. I scrolled through my snap-time for a while, and when hunger struck, I went to the kitchen. Before I could enjoy my meal, an idea popped into my head. I called Riva and informed her that Mom wouldn't be back until around 10 at night, and I was all alone. So, I invited her and Abir to my place for a Netflix and chill session, a mini house party!

"Hey, get something really delicious. Riva literally snatched the last piece of sandwich I had saved for myself, and I am starving now!" Abir said as he entered my home.

"Excuse me, I asked you, but you didn't respond, so I thought you must not be hungry! Stop crying now! Ana, please feed this little boy something. He only has two months left to enjoy *desi* Indian food. Who would bring this to you in Canada, by the way?" She interrupted.

"Relax, as soon as you guys confirmed, I immediately ordered pizzas for you, along with garlic bread and soft drinks. Just make sure Sneha doesn't find out!" I laughed.

"Oh, speaking of Sneha, Riva told me that your mom insisted you begin an internship in your Uncle's office. Is it true? You didn't tell me anything about it, and we just met yesterday." Abir asked and I immediately felt a storm of guilt coursing through my entire body.

Ultimately, I lied and said that I did mention the internship earlier, but he must have forgotten about it. He stood firm in his stand, expressing complete unawareness about this new beginning in my life. Riva stood by my side, trying to convince him that he had indeed forgotten about it.

"If both of you say so, fine. But how could I forget about your internship? I mean, throughout college, I encouraged you to start something, so it's a little difficult to digest the fact that I forgot about it. Anyway, where are you doing this? Is it like a regular office job? Tell me everything about it." He asked, intrigued.

"Okay, so, the office is about twenty minutes away from our college. I'm doing it mainly for my dad's sake. The timings are quite flexible for the first month. Is that enough information?" I hesitated, not wanting to disclose too much.

"Guys, I guess the pizza just arrived! No more serious stuff, let's just eat and enjoy."

"Oh with serious stuff I remember someone not-so-serious, I mean Kartik of course. Did he reach out to you after that incident?" Abir inquired. I was caught in a dilemma about how to respond because unintentionally, he was touching on a subject I was trying hard to keep guarded. Hesitant, I shared that Kartik had sent lengthy apology messages and was requesting to meet me. Despite my efforts to paint a positive image of Kartik, he remained unconvinced. He directly asked why I hadn't blocked him and why I was giving attention to what he saw as fake drama. Riva intervened and asked him why he held such strong animosity towards Kartik, to which he responded,

"I don't know! I just have this feeling that one day he will ruin everything we share! And will harm Ana."
"I mean, I have no concrete evidence for this, but I strongly believe it." he added.

I was torn, grappling with a spectrum of miserable emotions. Guilt gnawed at me for not being entirely truthful with Abir, while pity welled up for Kartik, whom I couldn't assist. Additionally, there was the sacrifice I made for my family by agreeing to the internship based on their wishes. Which emotion could I have pushed aside? Which deserved to take precedence? Or, which one could I have confided in Abir about? I knew he would be departing in just two to three months, but I had to stay here for the rest of my life.

The label of 'best friends' was always the one I cherished. It was the only tag that provided me with the kind of love I had always longed for. Committing to a romantic relationship has always brought me troubles. With Abir, I never felt the need for a boyfriend. However, that didn't mean he was my boyfriend; he was my everything, my best friend. Yes, I was apprehensive about entering into a romantic relationship with him *because I knew it could either be the most profound and serious relationship of my life or the most traumatic one. I couldn't risk what we have for what I wanted. What if I lost everything in the end?* Moreover, even if I contemplated something significant, what was the point if he was going to move across the country in the coming months? Was I prepared for another long-distance ordeal? Such friendships or relationships are like two parallel tracks, and perhaps, I wasn't suited to navigate either of them.

The torrent of thoughts seemed unending, but thankfully, the day concluded without my mother discovering that Abir had joined me in her absence. I slept well that night, but the upcoming week brought a rollercoaster of experiences during my internship.

After three days of relentless hard work, I received disheartening news—I hadn't managed to bring about a significant change in the advertisement program. The disappointment weighed heavily on my shoulders; only I knew how much effort and dedication I had poured into that project. It was disheartening to witness others discouraging me. With teary eyes, I sought solace in the canteen, and there I found Kartik enjoying tea and sandwiches.

"Ana, are you crying?" he asked.

"How does it matter to you? This is your dad's institute, right? That gives you full liberty to take a day off, miss deadlines, fail at projects, or do nothing! Still, nobody will question you. But just because I am an intern, that doesn't mean everybody can treat me like their punching bag." I yelled and cried and by the end of my mini dramatic monologue, I didn't realize what the fuck I did.

Kartik firmly held my hand and guided me straight to his dad's office. I tried to stop him, insisting him to reconsider, but he paid no heed and continued, marching us directly to Uncle Sushant's cabin.

"Dad, what's going on? Why is Ana being penalized for no apparent reason? She put in a lot of hard work!" he voiced his concerns.

"Please ignore him, Uncle. He's just being a bit too reactive." I interrupted.

"Kartik, you are the root cause of this. On the very first day, this task was assigned to pairs. You were absent, leaving her in a difficult position. Taking a stand for your colleague is good, but it's pointless unless you support them practically. She's new in this workspace, and the only person who could guide her is you. So, try to resolve the problem rather than creating a fuss."

His father's words began to make sense to him. After we exited the cabin, he apologized to me for his irresponsibility and careless attitude. He later reassured me that we would work together on the website and make it a success. I smiled, knowing he was trying to assist me, although he didn't realize he was helping himself. Later, I sent a message to his dad, apologizing for Kartik's behavior, but to my surprise, he was pleased that his son had finally taken an interest in the office after so long.

We dedicatedly worked on the website for two weeks and then fine-tuned it in the third. During this time, I missed college immensely. I made it a point to meet Abir every weekend and spend some *me-time* with him.

Ya ya I miss him..YES. I. MISS. HIM.

There were instances when I accompanied him to the Oberoi Immigration Office to provide support and be by his side throughout the process.

"I never knew you were so adept at multitasking. I mean, just look at how well you're managing your institute along with college." he remarked.

"It's been more than three weeks since I've been avoiding college, Abir." I responded.

"When I mentioned college, I meant me, silly! Initially, I thought this internship was an excuse to distance you from me even further. But now I understand that you're feeling guilty about leaving a friend like me, right?" He chuckled and winked at me.

"Jokes aside, you've helped me a lot—sometimes with your physical presence at the immigration office and other times with your emotional support to ease my burdening thoughts. I promise the first person I'll share every update with upon reaching Canada will be you, just YOU!" he expressed.

His words, meant to provide comfort, began to weigh on me. The more affectionate he became,-more the guilt grew from hiding things from him. But how could I tell him the truth when I knew it was too late, and we only had one month left to spend together? The second month would be consumed by exams, and then he would be gone. Would he truly leave?

Chapter 12

Let me comfort you.

With every passing month, the thought of parting ways from Abir grew more intense. The pressure inside my chest was making it difficult to breathe. What will I do once he actually leaves? On April 4th, I decided to take a day off from the institute and went to college for assignment submission and to catch up on some missed practicals. I informed Riva about my plan, and we both headed to the library to complete our clearances. To our surprise, Abir was already there, despite telling me he wouldn't be attending college that day.

"When Riva told me that you would be coming to college, I decided to tag along with you guys as well. Otherwise, what would you have done without me?" he laughed.

I was genuinely happy for his surprise, and an idea to surprise him back popped into my head. I texted Riva about it, and she agreed. While we were in the library, we saw Saloni ma'am, who was looking for the registered candidates for the Anthology competition. I tried to hide, but Abir shouted my name and informed the teacher that I was there.

"I won't spare you after this!" I said, playfully scolding him.

"Ananya, where have you been these days? Every other candidate has at least talked to me once, and they've all started writing their poems. But there has been no response from your side. You know you can't back off from this! I will impose a heavy fine!" she said.

"Ma'am I will try my best to submit it before the deadline."

"Just to remind you that from May 1st to May 31st, you have your end semester exams, and 5 months after that, you would be required to submit a soft copy of your work, late entries wouldn't be accepted. Okay?"

With these instructions, Saloni ma'am left and told me to be more focused and serious towards the competition.

"Ana, come on, at least start something. I'm here to encourage you, provide you with good ideas, and would also be there to listen to your thoughts. What else does a writer need?" Abir said.

You. I wanted to say you, that's what I need.

"Really? And what about after these two months? Will you call me day and night from Canada? No, right? Then just stay quiet, yaar! You literally dragged me into this mess. But I have a great solution. I just need to tolerate this teacher for one more month, then exams, and why would I come to college again? Of course, I won't pick up her calls. I think things will be sorted, right?"

The three of us shared amusing glances towards each other and headed to the canteen. Abir started inquiring about my internship, but I decided to keep him on hold. Since everything was going perfectly, I told him to stay calm and focus on his farewell month. He corrected me that he had two more months in Delhi, but we told him that one month would simply be consumed by the exams. Therefore, we decided to make April his "*Goodbye Eve Month.*" Riva told Abir to meet us at the café near NSP in the evening to spend his memorable times with us.

5 pm, café Philano,

We organized a cake cutting along with some small, thoughtful gifts. Knowing Abir's love for art, I made a mini cartoon featuring the three of us on a small canvas and decided to gift him. The drawing was far from perfect, and a bit messy, but I had tried to pour my all of my heartfelt and genuine emotions into it. Undoubtedly, the feeling that your best friend is on the path to success fills you with joy. However, when that success necessitates a distance between you, it becomes all the more heart-wrenching.

Before Abir could step in, I ordered his favorite items along with Riva, and we eagerly waited to see his reaction. It was the first time we had done something like this for him. As time went on, even Riva was becoming quite emotional. She had a different equation with Abir. They were friends before they met me, and that's how the three of us later became best-friends. Unlike Abir and me, they had several disagreements, but somehow, they always managed to sort things out by the end of the day. The three of us were indeed so attached to our story of how we met and continued to live the best life possible. However, we were too nervous that, like many other stories, our friendship might just be relegated to memories, confined to calls on birthdays and New Year's.

As Abir entered, he was shocked to see so many items on the table, not knowing that we had previously ordered this food for the three of us.

"Chill, it's on us." She laughed.

"We wish you a huge success and this cute little painting, of course. Whether you like it or not, you are still required to keep it and hang it in your hostel room to remind you that two silly pretty girls will always be there for you. Forever and ever." I smiled.

Abir hugged me, and that feeling when I hugged him back was priceless. That hug didn't witness any tears, but only smiles—a smile reminding us of all the precious memories we had made, the crazy times we had spent and the promises we had given.

A throat cleared behind us, "Guys, can you please make it a group hug and not make me feel like a third wheel, please?" The trio hug was my much-needed therapy. Years of shared joy, sorrow, dreams, and support culminated in it. We were standing there with our arms around each other, and I was overcome with thankfulness and love. I was comforted by the fact that, despite the impending physical separation between us, our bond would stay unbroken in that embrace. It served as a reminder that genuine friendships last a lifetime and exist only in the warm embrace of the heart. Every squeeze of that hug left a memory, a reminder of our steadfast friendship, and a source of power for the difficulties that were ahead. We made a quiet commitment to support one another no matter where life took us.

"Dare you not forget us!" I said facing the knife towards him. Before Abir could have answered, Riva started to laugh and added, "What if a real pretty girl approached you there? Don't hide it from me at least, okay?"

"Let him concentrate on his studies at least!" I said and it came out harsher than intended. But image of Abir with someone else on his arm, making him smile and sharing their secrets, made me want to gag.

"Well, you never know. Girls here never really liked me, maybe somebody will?" He added to Riva's laughter.

We continued with our meals and he showed us images of his university, hostel, and other things. Meanwhile, my mom called and started inquiring about my whereabouts, I managed to keep her on hold but my frustration was visible to Abir. He took away my phone and told me to start confronting realities with my mom rather than lying always.

"My mom isn't as cool as yours, Abir!"

"Get married; you'll have a cool mom too."

"Shut up."

"Look somebody is blushing." Riva added to my embarrassment.

"Will stay single than marrying an idiot like you, okay?" I tried mocking him and making faces. Inside I died a little death after uttering those non-sense words. *What the hell was I thinking?*

The surprise mini lunch date ended and like this, we arranged three more hangouts at different cafes where we enjoyed ourselves a lot and tried so much food along with nostalgic games like UNO and Chess. I was sidelining the internship a bit during April because I was more focused on spending time with Abir. However, Kartik didn't like it much as he thought I disappointed him by being irregular at the office. To my surprise, he called my dad and sugarcoated my hardwork to him, which in real I wasn't even doing at the office. My dad started doubting me but thanks to my witty brain who cleared his misconceptions. I immediately asked Kartik to meet near the sports complex .

"Kartik, are you out of your mind? What was the need to involve my dad in this?"

"I am sorry, I felt quite impulsive yesterday and that is why I did that. II knew you were busy with your stuff, I just wanted to do you something good. Ana, I am suffering from a mood disorder, along with anger issues and self-harm tendencies. I just can't help it. Since the day I have been seeing the lady in my dreams, I just find it extremely difficult to sleep!"

As he shared his struggle, I gently probed for more details about this haunting lady and the reasons behind her presence. What I found revealed a deeper issue underlying Kartik's troubled behavior.

"I had planned a group trip with my three friends. Unfortunately, all three had canceled for various reasons, leaving me disheartened. I didn't inform my dad and decided to go solo. Already frustrated and annoyed, I drove at an unacceptable speed. To avoid the heavy traffic on the main road, I took a shortcut through a slum area, about an hour away from my residence in Saharanpur. Then...

"I failed to notice the lady approaching. My car accidentally collided with her. Trust me, it was not intentional. Why would I inflict harm on someone? You know I'm not capable of such cruelty, right?" his voice quivered, his hands trembling. I reached out, holding his hand, gently rubbing it, urging him to stay calm. Swiftly, I got water for him, encouraging him to take a sip and continue with his account.

"I was utterly terrified, and I drove back home immediately. Throughout the journey, I felt a haunting presence, as if a soul was following me, urging me to either return or face eternal damnation. I screamed alone in the car, pleading to be spared, even though I knew there was nobody in the car with me. Within a few hours, news broke about a car striking a lady. Thankfully, my number plate wasn't visible, but I knew the truth. I felt utterly vulnerable as the public indirectly expressed their hatred towards me. A day later, I revisited the site and witnessed her family performing funeral rituals. I felt shattered, Ana. I had taken a life! Can you comprehend that? Kartik, a lady-killer! She won't let me find peace. She visits my dreams every alternate day, talking to me about death and suicide." He broke down in tears, the burden of guilt and fear weighing heavily on him.

I couldn't hold back the impulse to embrace him, expressing my gratitude for sharing the heavy load of his emotions. He went on to explain that this very narrative was the reason he shied away from seeking therapy; the thought of laying out everything and facing the potential consequences deterred him. I did my best to reassure him that therapy is confidential and that he need not fear divulging anything, especially to his father.

"You're the second person I've shared this entire story with; the first was my closest friend from Saharanpur. He has always stood by me."

Sometimes, life seems deeply unfair. People often say that a simple "sorry" can mend things, but no one mentions how accepting your mistakes before apologizing can heal you from within. Kartik, for instance, faced the harsh truths of his past—his mistakes, his irreversible actions. That acceptance made him feel a bit lighter, at least for a day.

Why is seeking therapy still stigmatized? Therapists are like doctors; they keep your secrets safe. I remember Kartik offering me tea on my first day at the office, telling me that some things are necessary even if we don't like them. When I shared this with him, he surprised me with a hug. Words escaped me as I held the once stoic Kartik, now sobbing on my shoulder like a child. I hugged him back, purely to comfort him, and trust me, it was an 'only-comforting-friend-hug.

You know," he whispered through his tears, "I've never felt this vulnerable before."

"It's okay," I replied softly, "sometimes being vulnerable is the strongest thing you can do."

Chapter 13

Approaching the end?

I vividly recall that day, one of the final weeks of April, just before my scheduled break for May. The task assigned to me was undeniably challenging. I was stationed in the admission department, tasked with calling leads individually within a strict 30-minute timeframe. In total, there were 40 leads, and my goal was to introduce them to the institute and entice them to visit our office for further details. By the time I had finished contacting 20 clients, exhaustion had taken its toll. Kartik, seated nearby, inquired, "Is there an issue?"

"Even if there is, I have nobody to help me out." I replied in frustration.

"I'm well-versed with this work. But why would I help you?" he taunted with a smirk.

"I don't even want your help. Who knows, you might mess up the task. So, stay away."

Nonetheless, he proceeded to take the client list upon himself and efficiently completed the rest of the work. Out of the 20 remaining clients, he managed to convince 8 to visit our institute. I was genuinely impressed. I shot him a glance of approval and appreciation, raising my eyebrows, which noticeably boosted his spirits. When his father walked into our cabin and witnessed us working together, he was visibly delighted. I informed him that Kartik had assisted me, and he could hardly believe his ears. It had been quite some time since he had done something substantial for the office.

His dad approached me and said, "Furthermore, you've requested leave for the entire month of May due to the end-semester exams. After that, you'll be returning to the institute, correct?

"In addition to that, your performance has been reviewed, and you'll be a salaried employee starting from June. Congratulations, Ana!"

The words from his dad filled me with joy. Never had I imagined that I would receive such appreciation for any work and will start earning immediately after graduation. When I shared this update with Mom, she danced with joy. Her dream of seeing her daughter become successful finally took a step. I also called Abir and Riva to tell the same; they were thrilled to hear it. Surprisingly, Abir asked both of us to meet near the institute and celebrate this update. I managed to sneak out during the break, and both of them made the hour special for me.

They ordered pasta and pizza, and extended their wishes for my future success. I was surprised by Abir's presence since he seldom organizes outings right before exams. It meant a lot to me that he bent his usual rules and took the time to join in my celebration.

"What's the worst that could happen if I lose a few marks for a question? But there's so much at stake if I lose out on these moments. I don't want to regret later that I spent my last few days in Delhi the wrong way." He assured with a smile.

"What do you mean?"

"Jab pata ho ki waqt kamm hai, toh bache hue waqt ko sahi se bita lena chahiye. Kyunki jab ye waqt beet jayega, toh sirf yaaden hi rahe jayengi."

"When you know that time is short, you should make the most of the remaining moments. Because once this time passes, only memories will endure." He replied.

Remember *Naina* from *YJHD*, *"kitna bhi try karlo bunny life me kuch na kuch to chhootega hi"* I felt exactly that. He was missing his classes to celebrate with me. Meanwhile me, I was just lying and lying to my one and only ABIR.

I smiled as we let the comforting silence embrace us. Riva broke the quietude, reminding us of Abir's upcoming birthday, almost 20 days away. I mentally smacked my head at how I could forget, and it turned out he had forgotten too. We decided that the three of us would make his 22nd birthday an unforgettable one, leaving the choice of venue to Riva and me.

"I wonder if you'll be celebrating your 23rd birthday with us, right." I teased, a playful smirk on my face.

"Just a reminder, I'll be leaving for Canada on 4th June, and I'll be back within 8 months. So, even if I can't be here on my birthday, we'll celebrate it in advance, okay?" he chuckled.

Later, he started asking about my internship and job profile, making me nervous as he was still unaware of the details. Every time I tried to tell him in the past, something came up and I was pulled back. With only a month left, I decided it wasn't worth creating a fuss.

I wanted him only for myself, no Kartik, no moving. Just me and him. Every day, this need to stay close to him and spend my most, was growing at an irrational rate. I still can't decipher my emotions exactly what is this pull towards. This wasn't some platonic pull like of a baby's pull towards their favourite cousin because they gave them gifts, but this pull was like that of a lover when they see their beloved. Just like we read in books. That itch to hug him and stay there. That feeling of HOME. One thing had become clear; WE WERE DEFINITELY MORE THAN just FRIENDS.

Riva came to my rescue, diverting the conversation. I left for the office and got back to work. While dealing with leads, my mind couldn't help but plan the birthday.

With my meagre savings, I resolved to organize the best birthday bash for him. The day ended on a good note as I bid farewell to my colleagues, who also wished me luck with my exams. Kartik seemed disappointed at my decision to take a break and urged me to return to work as soon as possible. I encouraged him to stay committed and responsible at work. Thus, my journey as an intern concluded. As May rolled on, I began preparing for my exams, and it proved to be an exhausting month. Being a somewhat lackadaisical student during college, the challenge of covering everything by the night before the exams was daunting. Fortunately, two of my exams went relatively well by mid-May, and it was time to focus on celebrating Abir's birthday. Alongside Riva, I busied myself with the preparations.

Chapter 14

Birthday bash babe.

Celebrating Abir's birthday meant more to us than just a typical event; it was a chance to express our love, appreciation, and thoughtfulness towards him. The idea of crafting a unique birthday experience for my closest friend stemmed from the treasure trove of shared memories and the desire to add another unforgettable chapter. Planning meticulously was essential to make this event genuinely special and meaningful.

We wanted to ensure that his happiness was at the core of the celebration. Riva and I brainstormed and designed a full-day outing centred around art and adventure. We settled on a nearby famous nursery park with a tranquil ambiance, providing an ideal backdrop for adventure-themed activities. We also booked a room for us in the *Riyash Hotel* where we asked them to do the preparations in advance.

Simultaneously, we prepared gifts for Abir, encapsulating our love and memories. Among these were a beautifully bound travel journal and a scrapbook filled with cherished moments from our years of friendship.

Walking into the *Riyash Hotel*, the staff welcomed us with genuine warmth and care, offering their assistance at every step. Abir was taken aback by the exquisite decoration adorning the entire room - vibrant balloons, streamers, and a massive banner that read *"Happy Birthday"* alongside another one saying *"We Will Miss You Forever"*. Overwhelmed by the thoughtful gesture, he sat beside me, got teary eyes and locked those precious beautiful eyes with me, expressing his all the love silently.

"I love you. I mean I really love you both. You guys made my day so special," he said, his voice filled with weary emotions.

"HAPPY BIRTHDAY, ABIR!" we cheered, our hearts brimming with joy at having made our best friend's day so extraordinary. He was genuinely touched by our efforts.

"If your best friends can love you this much, do you even need a partner? It makes you wonder, right?" he mused, looking at us with gratitude. Riva pulled out three beer cans, and we marked cheers.

I surprised Abir with a video I had put together with all my heart, a montage of our memories from school days to college. The video had all our pictures, and he was overjoyed watching it. He kept pausing at every moment, reminiscing about the beautiful memories linked to each image. He even paused at the diary he had gifted me and asked if I still wrote in it.

"Not currently, but I know I'll definitely need it when you leave."

"Paper is way better than a human." he quoted **Anne Frank**, smiling.

"You know, it was all Ana's idea. She wanted your farewell to be the best, and she even wrote a farewell speech for you!" Riva chimed in.

"But before that, can we please have our food? I'm dying to dig into this pizza!" she added, her enthusiasm is contagious.

Within a few minutes, our table was adorned with an array of delightful dishes. We indulged in pizza, cigar rolls, noodles, and Coke, and an assortment of other delectable treats, leaving not a single morsel behind. After our feast, we created some fun videos, played lively music, and danced to our hearts' content. He expressed his eagerness to hear the farewell speech I had prepared for him. Shyness crept over me initially, but with both of them persistently urging me to share, I gathered my courage, took out the sheet, and began:

"Looking back to the place where I met you for the first time, I would curse the school that gave me a cringe, lame, and stupid friend like you. But I will forever be thankful that the same place had given me somebody as special as you. From the moment we became friends, our journey has been an incredible adventure filled with laughter, love, and shared dreams. You have been my pillar of strength, my confidant, and my partner in all of life's ups and downs. Your unwavering support and encouragement have lifted me in moments of doubt and kept me grounded when the world felt chaotic.

I get annoyed every time you roast me, but I will forever miss that roasting. I get upset at you for not listening to my tantrums, but I would forever miss taunting you. I would miss you coming to my place secretly hoping that one day you would come and surprise me with a bouquet saying, 'I am back, Ananya.'

The numerous times you've made me grin, including late-night discussions, impromptu road excursions, and silent moments of understanding. I cherish every moment, and I am incredibly appreciative of the love and happiness you have brought into my life.

As we bid farewell, let it be known that this marks the inception of a fresh chapter in your life. I firmly assert that in this chapter, the spotlight should only be on two central characters - your best friend, that is, me, and, naturally, Riva. We have been, we are, and we ought to continue being significant in your life. I know we would be living physically apart, but I hope that this trio would be inseparable. I have faith that our separation will only strengthen our love, just as we have done in the past when we overcame difficulties together."

As I concluded my speech, I witnessed Abir's eyes welling up with tears, a kaleidoscope of emotions swirling within him. It was as if he was riding an emotional rollercoaster, reliving the tapestry of memories we had woven over the years. He listened to every word so attentively, so deeply, that I felt an intense connection and attachment to him. I found myself falling for the beauty of being truly heard. With each sentence, a rush of flashbacks washed over him—moments of joy, struggles, growth, and shared adventures. It was as if I had delicately woven the threads of our lives into a vibrant tapestry that now hung before us, a living testament to our journey.

All three of us were swept away by a tide of emotions. As I wiped away a tear, I realized that these emotions would remain forever etched in my heart, a reminder of the beautiful resonance that unfolds when words are spoken from the depths of one's soul.

"Jaana zaruri hai kya?" Abir said while looking towards me. (Is it necessary to leave?)

I nodded, a bittersweet smile on my face. Abir reciprocated with a reassuring smile. He took me by my elbow and hugged me like his life depended on it, squeezing the soul out of me. We hugged, knowing deep down that these hugs were becoming a rarity. I was grateful for every shared moment, yet the looming reality of our impending separation weighed heavily on my heart.

"I'm sorry, Abir, for taking our time together for granted. Today, as you prepare to leave, I realize that nobody remains forever. I've let you down at times, and now, I wish for more moments with you." I confessed, my voice tinged with regret.

"We still have so much time ahead! Trust me, our bond won't waver an inch even if I am in the other end of the world." he reassured me, attempting to soothe my anxious heart and his as well. Amid our emotional exchange, we revisited past escapades, laughter mingling with tears. He was curious about the excuse I had given my mother for our day out, and I confessed I had fabricated a story about an office practical to put her at ease. Otherwise, she would have scolded me for bunking work.

"You're turning 22 and still lying to your mom! That's not good." Riva teased, lightening the moment with her playful remark.

"The stricter the parents, the more spoiled the kids are! I mean, look at you, holding beers and glasses, and your mom thinks that you are having your practical right now!" he laughed.

"By the way, it's just 15 days now. Have you started packing?" Riva interrupted, steering the conversation towards his imminent departure. He mentioned that his mom was assisting with the packing, allowing him to focus on his exams. He would have three days after the last exam to wrap up the last-minute preparations before moving.

Abir excitedly showed us detailed pictures of his hostel in Canada and other intriguing things. After a while, the three of us booked a cab to a nearby nursery, immersing ourselves in the soothing weather and embracing nature. Though I wasn't particularly fond of clouds or greenery, that day, I found myself enjoying everything that brought Abir happiness.

Amidst the laughter and good times, as we indulged in nachos and beer, I gathered the courage to broach a topic I hadn't prepared for. It's time. *Now or never.* "I know this might sound a bit lame and immature, and honestly, I don't think I've done anything to deserve it, but..." I began, feeling a bit nervous.

"Can we go on a date? I'll plan everything, and I'd really appreciate your presence." I stammered out, hoping he'd understand the sincerity behind my request.

"Is third-wheeling allowed?" Riva chimed in playfully.

"I'm in!" he immediately responded as if he was waiting for this from a lifetime.

"A proper, uninterrupted date this time! No disturbances, no chaos, and sorry, no Riva!" he added, and we all laughed, the prospect of the upcoming date lightening the mood.

We mutually decided that two days before he leaves for Canada, i.e., on 2nd July, we would be going on a date. I don't know if any context like, "just friends date" existed by then, *because it definitely was something we were looking for.*

"2nd July, we are going on a date, right?"

I nodded, "It's a date". And the day ended smoothly.

Wait, did it really? Did that just happen? Am I going on a date? With Abir?

Oh my god.. OH. MY. GOD.

As I stepped into my home, I sensed something was off. Mom was giving me a deadly look, and Dad was conspicuously absent. I tried to navigate my way to my room, attempting to stay silent.

"How was the practical exam, Ananya?" she asked, her tone laced with an undercurrent of suspicion. "Great! How else could it have been?" "Must have been tiring, waiting for your turn amidst 70 students in the class, right?" she prodded, attempting to keep the conversation going.

"Yes, that's why I got late. Riva had a very poor practical, and..." I started to explain.

"Sakshi called for you. She wanted to update you regarding an internship. When I told her you were at the practical, she mentioned there was no practical today. Unfortunate for her to miss an important event, isn't it?" Mom said. I felt a surge of frustration at her habit of intertwining things and never getting straight to the point. I finally erupted, bluntly admitting that yes, I had lied. Not just that day, but many times before because I didn't believe she could handle the truth.

"Every facet of my life seemed predetermined by you. I never had the chance to chart my course because you and Dad always made the decisions for me. Do you ever wonder why your daughter is so unaware of the world's ways? It's because I was never allowed to try anything on my own. I understand I'm not remarkable in any way; I'm just an ordinary, average girl from a middle-class background. But that's my burden, not yours!" I vented my frustration, tears rolling down my cheeks.

"You chose my school, my college, my workplace—everything for me! And now? Can't I even deviate from a single obligation without you knowing? What if I told you I went to my friend's birthday and his farewell today? Would you have let me go? Obviously not! So, Mom, let me have a taste of freedom." I declared sprinting towards my room, before closing the door with a deep breath. I wasn't ready to face my mom anymore, my eyes were moist, and the mascara smeared my tears.

Unexpectedly, I received a call from Kartik, but I declined it and continued crying. He even texted me twice, but I was not in any condition to tell him anything. *I wanted Abir.* He is only one to handle me and he is the only one who truly and completely understands me.

It became crystal clear that nobody in the whole world could bridge the chasm of understanding and conflicting emotions that existed between my mother and me. The gap seemed insurmountable, a deep crevice of differences in perspectives and a struggle for autonomy. The more we tried to communicate, the further apart we seemed to drift, our words and intentions lost in the churning sea of misunderstandings and unspoken sentiments. It was a realization that hit me like a tidal wave, making me comprehend that this was a battle only we could fight, and it would take time and patience, and perhaps, still, we would never be on the same page

In the weeks that followed, our interactions became sparse. Dad attempted to intervene, but his efforts seemed futile. Finally, the day of our last exam arrived, coinciding with our "scribble day." Armed with markers and t-shirts, we wrote heartfelt messages on each other's tees.

"Just friends?" was scribbled on my tee-shirt. A smile spread across my face; I was fairly certain who had written it. *Abir.* Yet, there's a beauty in quietly cherishing gestures, in allowing unsaid feelings to weave their own tales. The day was an emotional rollercoaster for us, a trio whose bond was deeply rooted in years of shared memories and laughter during our time in college. We had spent more time together outside of college classrooms, often skipping classes to be in each other's company. Those were the moments that defined the best times of my college days.

Before we decided to part our ways, I stopped Abir and asked him, "Venice mall, tomorrow? You'll be there, right?"

"Do you think I could say no?

"It's always a yes when it comes to you," he added.

Never in this world had I imagined asking Abir on a date, but some things are best experienced when they flow naturally. No planning, no overthinking—just going with the flow. Perhaps fate was attempting to bring us closer, but I wondered if it had waited too long. I had waited to long.

Chapter 15

And yes, a date.

The clock chimed eleven in the afternoon when Abir urgently summoned me to meet him at Pitampura metro station. I was dressed in a pristine white one-piece outfit, complemented by nude heels and flowing hair. My makeup was subtle, and I adorned a pair of earrings that accentuated my attire. Excitement filled me as I prepared to leave the house, but my enthusiasm was interrupted by my mother's inquiry:

"When do you plan to be back?"

"Can't you just let me go this once?" I retorted, frustration evident as I shut the door and took a deep breath.

I despised last-minute interruptions, especially from someone named *Sneha*, but it seemed impossible to thwart a concerned mother. After confirming my meeting plans with Abir, we both reached the designated spot at almost the same time.

To my surprise, he had arrived in his mom's car, an unusual occurrence given that she rarely permitted him to use it. Later, I discovered that he had pleaded with his mom to share the car keys, emphasizing how important it was for the date to be perfect in every way. As I settled into the car, I noticed Abir was also wearing a white t-shirt, a delightful and unexpected twinning of outfits. He even complimented the coincidence with a cheerful yellow rose.

"A yellow rose?" I thought to myself.

Of course, he thinks we are just friends because I rejected him like a fool. I want to kill myself.

"I could have given you a red one." he explained, "but I understand this is a one-day date from your perspective. So, yellow rose it is." he added, flashing a warm smile.

Throughout the journey, romantic songs played, adding to the enchanting atmosphere. We relished the music and exchanged shy yet endearing glances, each one making me blush a little more. However, before we approached the mall, a sudden craving for hot coffee struck me. I scanned the surroundings, but no café or shop seemed to be in sight. I assured Abir not to worry and suggested we head straight to the mall. Soon, he pulled over at an unknown destination, leaving me curious and eager to find out his intentions. For the next twenty minutes, my curiosity grew, and I persistently questioned him about our destination. However, he remained tight-lipped, urging me to be patient and trust him.

"You were craving coffee, right?" he remarked, parking the car with a mischievous grin.

"Yes, but I couldn't spot a café nearby." I replied, puzzled by his unexpected stop.

"This is where my mom and I used to spend evenings." he shared, a hint of nostalgia in his voice. "It's not a lavish or exciting, theme-based café. It's been here since I was eight, and amazingly, nothing has changed. It's like a low-key, stable zone for me. But of course, feel free to enjoy your coffee and maybe some Maggie if you like."

The air was infused with the delightful aroma of freshly brewed coffee and the tempting scent of pastries. Nestling into a cozy corner, we were greeted by the warm, inviting ambiance—soft lighting and comfortable seating encouraged us to relax and take our time. I can see why this is his favourite. It's so quiet and peaceful. *Just like him.* Sipping our favourite beverages, we swapped stories and shared laughter, our merriment blending with the gentle clink of cups, creating a melodic harmony that felt almost magical.

After putting our cups back down, Abir directed me to return to the car as we headed towards our final destination—Venice Mall. During the journey, my phone buzzed incessantly with calls and messages from Kartik, but I chose to completely ignore him. I craved an undisturbed, authentic experience with Abir. I sent Kartik a text, informing him that I was on my way to Venice Mall with a friend.

After silencing my phone, Abir noticed my focused silence and began to inquire if everything was alright. I nodded, offering a reassuring smile. Soon, we arrived at the mall, he parked the car, and we excitedly stepped into the Venice-themed mall. I told him that I had booked tickets for a movie as well. I could see shyness enveloping him as we knew this movie would be special for us—it would mark the first time we were watching a movie together as a *date*.

Our destination was more than just a shopping complex; it was a place where memories would be made, laughter would echo, and connections would deepen. With anticipation fluttering in the air, we set out for a delightful date at the mall.

The chaotic atmosphere of the mall welcomed us. A symphony of sensory delights was generated by the lively hum of people, the melodic music playing in the background, and the enticing fragrances from the adjacent restaurants. As we walked hand in hand, anticipation for a good evening flashed in our eyes.

Abir held my hand and hurried me towards Zafia- a very expensive brand of perfumes. I told him that I had no budget for a perfume at that moment, but he had a different thought. He asked to buy a common perfume for both of us.

"You know what I love about Zafia is that no matter how hard you try, once you apply their perfume, the fragrance lingers on." he said.

"In a similar way, I expect that the fragrance of our relationship never fades away, even if I move to Canada. You don't trust me? Fine. You don't trust yourself? Fine. But I can't believe that you don't trust us! The same 'us' whom everybody has been admiring for years. I know you haven't verbalized anything in these months, but don't you think your eyes reveal the secrets you hold? I can't be wrong here." he added earnestly.

"I think I can't handle a long-distance relationship with just anyone. You are a real gem, and..." I trailed off, my thoughts muddled with my biggest fear of Long-Distance. Abir nodded understandingly, encouraging me to move forward and smile a bit.

We proceeded to purchase two perfumes, making a promise to each other to never fade away, much like those perfumes. As we continued our journey through the mall, my eyes caught sight of a boating activity—*the Gondola ride*— within the mall itself.

There were three boats in total, and each boat was a masterpiece, adorned with intricate carvings, plush cushions, and a gondolier donning a traditional striped shirt and straw hat. It was a scene that seemed straight out of a dream, and we couldn't wait to step aboard.

The gondolier gracefully handled the waterways as we nestled into the gondola, his oar strokes generating a rhythmic song that set the tone for our ride. The peace surrounded us, and the noise and bustle of the city felt worlds away. The smooth rocking of the boat and the lullaby of the water against its sides produced a tranquil and enchanting atmosphere. Couples and families waved as they passed by on their gondola journeys, creating a sense of camaraderie and shared joy. The atmosphere was one of happiness, relaxation, and the sheer pleasure of escaping the ordinary for a little while.

Abir was captivated, constantly snapping pictures of me, his gaze never wavering from my face. The gondolier couldn't help but smile at us, offering to take a picture of us together. He clicked a beautiful shot, which I kept secretly in my hidden album, a cherished memory. I reached out and dipped my fingers into the water, feeling its coldness. Abir gently took my hand within his, submerged in the water, and gazed at me tenderly. As his eyes locked with mine, I couldn't help but blush, the warmth of his touch and the intensity of his gaze sending a delightful shiver down my spine. Unexpectedly, our boat encountered a technical issue, leaving us stranded in the middle of the water. The others in the boat started to panic, but surprisingly, I remained remarkably calm.

"Are you not feeling scared?" Abir asked.

"Maybe it's because of your presence that nothing seems to scare me. I know we'll find a way together, no matter the situation. Isn't that right?" I replied, smiling.

The boat started moving again, easing the tension. As our boating trip neared its end, a sense of fulfilment enveloped us. The event had been a beautiful blend of imagination and reality, a brief escape into a world of timeless romance. Disembarking with smiles on our faces and memories in our hearts, the gondolier escorted us back to the port. We left the quiet river with a sense of amazement and a common connection, eternally linked by the unique and wonderful journey we had shared in the heart of the city.

Before our movie, we couldn't resist the allure of the gaming zone—it was simply too enticing. The array of exciting games, including car racing, air hockey, bowling, bumper cars, and basketball, drew us in. We loaded a card with credits worth Rs.700 and dove into the gaming frenzy. We started with air hockey, where Abir outplayed me with ease, likely due to his practice with a mini version at home. Next up was a glass box filled with huge teddy bears. Abir gave it a shot, but luck wasn't on his side. I burst into laughter at his defeat, and in response, he challenged me to a basketball game. To his surprise, I showcased my skills and sunk shot after shot flawlessly.

"I guess I taught you this before. Right?" he chuckled.

I winked playfully and continued the game. We then hopped into bumper cars, revelling in the fun chaos, colliding with each other, playfully arguing about who drove better. Abir reminded me of the movie, but we still had an hour left, so I suggested we try bowling. Little did I know, it would present a challenge. The rules didn't permit us to play with our shoes on, and we had to try the socks instead.

Unfortunately, I was wearing the tightest shoes that day, making it impossible for me to remove them on my own. When I informed Abir about my predicament, he smiled and bent down to help.

"What are you doing? What will others think?" I panicked.

"Put your foot on my lap; I'll try to loosen the laces for you." he assured me.

He attempted to loosen the laces for me, but when that didn't work, he guided me to sit near a sofa and proceeded to assist. Doubts about embarrassment crept in, and I hesitated.

"Abir, I think we shouldn't do this. It's so embarrassing; people might be laughing at us."

"I don't care about others. All I care about is you want to go bowling, and nothing else matters! Just tilt your feet a little and try pushing it backward; in a minute, I'll get them out."

Following his instructions, both of my shoes were thankfully removed, and we proceeded to enjoy the activity. we were average at it, but we were enjoying every part of it. Two rounds were allocated to each player, and we made various empty and full shots too. We made videos of each other as well, and the game ended with equal scores for both of us. It was indeed a good time with him.

As the clock struck 3, I eagerly nudged Abir, signalling it was time for the movie, and we made our way into the PVR. Although I had been to movies with Abir before, this time felt different, more intimate, as it was just the two of us. We settled into our seats, and just as I began to immerse myself in the moment, my phone started ringing incessantly.

Three calls from my mom began to worry me. He suggested I send her a quick text about our whereabouts, but I hesitated, knowing how risky it could be.

"I'm in the middle of a movie with Riva. I'll call you as soon as this ends." I typed, mustering the courage to reply, and then decided to keep my phone on silent to avoid any more disturbances.

The movie began, and I realized I hadn't paid my share to Abir for the gaming zone. So I retrieved the cash and attempted to give it to him. He initially declined but then gently held my hand, suggesting we remain this way throughout the entire movie. My cheeks reddened as I obliged, resting my head on his shoulder.

"Can't this last forever? You and me, and the moments we share?" I whispered.

"You are that part of my life for which I would literally leave everything aside. Your 'yes' is all that matters, and trust me, nothing would change between us. You fear long distance, right? What if I decide to stay here? In fact, my mom is getting too emotional about me leaving her. I'm feeling unsure too, whether I should go or not. And I know it's never too late to make the right decision. But if I choose not to go, will you stay by me here?"

Abir's words hit me like a ton of bricks, and it felt as if the ground slipped from beneath me. I couldn't bring myself to make eye contact with him, so I leaned more on his shoulder, a tear escaping. He gently wiped it away, and we continued with the movie. An uneasy silence settled between us. Was this silence the result of a colossal mistake? The absence of words seemed to intensify our connection, as we communicated through shared glances. Thanks to a few punch lines in the movie that enabled us to settle a bit, laughing and gossiping about the story. He didn't leave my hand even for a second, and I too felt so relaxed and comfortable while resting my head on his shoulder.

During the intermission, the tempting aroma of buttered popcorn filled the air, teasing our senses. Abir asked if I wanted something to eat, but I declined, mindful of the high prices of food at the PVR. Meanwhile, he pulled out something from his pocket—a handcrafted pendant he had made.

That pendant looked so beautiful; it had a touch of resin and flower petals inside it. The platinum chain made it look even more attractive. It was a tear-shaped pendant with my initial crafted in it. I couldn't take my eyes off it; Abir had a marvellous command of art, and his skills blew my mind that day. We exchanged smiles, and I promised to keep the pendant safe forever.

"When an artist falls in love with a writer, the story becomes artistically beautiful, isn't it?" Abir mused.

"I am not a writer, though," I laughed, putting on the pendant he had crafted. Abir helped me tie it, and I sent a picture of it to Riva. As the movie began, he excused himself to use the restroom. In the interim, I checked my phone for any updates and was shocked to find 15 missed calls from Kartik. I quickly called him back, and his voice sounded incredibly tense.

"Ananya, have you lost your mind? I literally called you 15 times!"

"I'm sorry, my phone was on silent. What happened exactly?"

"I have a surprise for you! But before that, I am clearly upset that you tried knowing everything about me and my past but didn't let me know that you had relations with my closest friend- Ankush! That is why you always used to act hesitated whenever I talked about Aarvi, Saharanpur or..."

"Kartik, have you lost your mind? And who told you about me and Ankush?" I fumbled.

"Thankfully, I mentioned about you to Ankush. Remember the day I told you about the lady of my haunting dreams? I told you that apart from you, it was my closest friend who knew everything, right? So the friend is none other than Ankush. Look, you have done a lot for me Ana, it is because of you that I am doing well in office, I am into therapy too and I always wanted to do something good for you. I know Ankush loves you and you love him too, he was your first love. I mean he is. Please talk to him. We are the same location as yours."

MY GOD! KARTIK UNKNOWINGLY HARMED ME TO EVERY EXTENT POSSIBLE. HE LEFT ME SPEECHLESS.

I felt like, he forcefully made me re-read a chapter that would disrupt the current chapter I wanted to read, and not just that, he might simply end my book.

I felt everything was falling apart. I couldn't explain the situation to Abir, feeling like I was disappointing him yet again. Before I could figure out everything, he returned, accompanied by a staff member who brought us delicious food. "Sorry, but I knew you were hungry," he said with a warm smile.

I struggled to eat, knowing that the looming confrontation would ruin my appetite for days. This was not how I envisioned our date ending. Forget about relationship; I wasn't even loyal in our friendship. The same friendship that once made me feel so alive, cheerful, and lively, I had ended up breaking it into pieces. I didn't want to be so cruel to anyone. Or did I?

Within an hour, the movie concluded, and our date neared its end. We stepped outside the theatre. I tried my best to convince Abir to leave for our places, but innocent he, unaware of the chaos I had created, wanted to stay longer, spend time with me, and do some shopping. Before I could attempt to explain, everything shattered when I saw the two unwanted humans standing there, right in front of us. I couldn't even dare to look at Abir experiencing the betrayal. He ignored the guys and was constantly trying to make an eye-contact with me. Tears welled up in my eyes, and he understood the fishiness that settled over us.

"Please, Abir, I can explain." I begged.

"If I am not wrong, you told me that you were in touch with neither of them, right?"

"I did an internship at Kartik's institute. I will explain everything to you, I just need a chance."

"Remember when I said, 'Ananya, I am ready to leave everything aside only if you promise to stay by my side?' I actually meant it. Nevertheless, how could I ever expect loyalty from you?" His words were a knife to the heart. And I deserved it. I did ruin this for us.

Before I could say anything, Ankush interjected, "Listen, I just need to make things clear from my side. Can we step aside and talk about what happened? I need closure. It seems you've moved on, but I'm still standing there. On the same road where you left me alone."

"You left her, and she was still there. And now that she has moved on, you're dragging your stupid explanations here! My foot." Abir retorted.

"Brother, are you guys into a relationship?" Ankush's question made both of us silent and the silence got transformed into Abir's rage when Kartik interrupted saying,

"Ugh No. They are 'Just friends.'"

"It was Aarvi's birthday. I never wanted to go there because she just ditched Kartik then, my best friend. I tried hard to convince this asshole that there was no point in me attending her birthday party. But he was desperate to know the gossip. Everything got planned so suddenly that I had no time left to inform you about anything.

"While we were celebrating her birthday, she introduced us to Abhishek. They started dating a week ago, and in a very casual tone, she said that Abhishek never called her 'baby' the way Kartik used to call her. That was it. I was just replying to her in Kartik's style to remind her of him. Everyone was just mocking the whole thing, but you took it to a completely different level." He explained.

"Ankush. Firstly, it didn't matter. Secondly, it still doesn't matter. I don't give a fuck about you, Aarvi, Kartik, or fucking anyone from Saharanpur" I cried.

"Moreover, we were just stupid teenagers by then. Gaurav tried manipulating me against you a lot; that was the reason I never took the initiative to talk to you." he added.

"Fuck him for ruining our relationship. I knew it! I knew the asshole was him who misguided you. Trust me, I would kill him. But for now, I want to say something to you Ana. I know that I'm not the perfect prince charming guy for you, nor can I bring wonders into your life, but together we can make it better. I'm still here, waiting for the same Ananya that I met during high school. What distanced us was a misunderstanding, and what can bring us back is closure. I still love you, Ana. Fate finally made an excuse to bring us back together via Kartik. He worked hard to clear me everything, and now I think, no I know we can fix everything back to how it should be."

Ankush was the first guy I ever loved, the first guy I ever felt something for, the first guy for whom I lied. Kartik tried to convince me to forgive his friend and start everything afresh. I felt incredibly guilty for trusting someone else and jeopardizing my well-running relationship during high times. When I looked at Abir, he had no expressions; only his eyes had turned wet, and he was biting his lips to suppress the storm of emotions within him.

"Won't you say something?" I said.

"You know why I always asked you to distance yourself from Kartik? I used to tell you that I never got the right intentions from him. I knew he would show his true colors someday, and this is it. He became victorious in what he always wanted." Abir added.

"You have loved Ankush with all your heart. He was your first love. Could you forget him this easily without even giving him a chance? He has come all the way from Saharanpur to Delhi just to sort things out between the two of you." Kartik interrupted, disregarding Abir's words. I took a pause, feeling a wave of nostalgia for the memories of my first love. I couldn't gather the courage to look at my best friend and just whispered to him,

"Better luck, Abir, for your future. I hope you'll always shine."

He gave me a tough expression and just left—forever. I stood there, waiting for him to turn back, but he didn't. My eyes tried focusing on him for as long as they could, but eventually, I could see him no longer.

I left the place too, booked a cab and rushed back home.

I wondered if that day marked the moment I lost him if I had lost everything. Perhaps, I had done nothing to deserve him. I hid a lot, not wanting to disappoint him, but in the end, I disappointed him even more. The sad part about losing him was that it wasn't just him I lost, but also a piece of me. I felt frightened to face him again. Silly me had been dreaming of a life with him, not knowing that I couldn't even spend a day with him properly. I was devastated and withdrew from everyone. I stopped replying to Riva or anyone else. I knew that a day later, Abir would be gone forever, and then whatever we had would just disappear.

Tears welled up in my eyes as I sat alone, lost in the depth of my thoughts. It became 3 in the night; the room was silent, providing an escape for me to cry and vent out everything to myself. The weight of impending separation bore down on my heart, and I couldn't control myself at the mere thought of Abir leaving for abroad.

To make scenarios worse, I started scrolling through my gallery and realized that the same folders that were once filled with the warmth of our laughter and tender moments now seemed empty and desolate. Every picture held a memory, reminding me of all the beautiful days we had spent together, and it felt so fragile, as everything had ended too soon with his departure.

I tried to sleep to distract myself, at least for a few hours, but tears flowed unbidden down my cheeks. I started regretting that I couldn't even say goodbye to him. A part of me tried to assure me that it was just a temporary separation, but my mind knew that it was not. It tore my soul not knowing when or if we would ever be reunited. Would it be a matter of weeks, months, or even years? We would be separated by time zones and distance, but the pain of missing his presence already tore my heart and shattered my dreams.

Later, I told Riva not to contact me for a few days as I needed some space and time to process everything that happened between Abir and me. She insisted that I should talk to him once and at least settle things with a warm goodbye, but I had no courage to face my lost love.

Two days later, I received a message from Riva that Abir had left. I left her on read and tried to hold back my tears. In the daylight, I felt shattered and broken. I started shedding tears, and that was when mom entered and asked me what was wrong. I couldn't answer anything and continued crying. She hugged me tightly, and I felt relieved in her arms. She patted my back and said, "*Meri bahadur bachi hai tu toh.*" (You are my strong girl.)

I made eye contact with her and told her that I was okay; it was just a fight between me and Riva.

"Till how long are you going to excuse Riva for Abir?" she smiled.

"You think that I don't understand you, that I don't get you, and that I don't like you. But whatever you say, I am your mom, after all. You would hide a hundred things from me, and I would know all of it. But the only reason I stayed quiet is for you not to feel embarrassed. On your Naani's death, I heard your conversation with Ankush as well, but I didn't say anything. I knew you secretly used to visit his place keeping Daisy as an excuse. Similarly, these few months have been about you lying about Abir with Riva as an excuse, isn't it? I always wished that you could come straight to me and confront all your problems because I might give you a logical solution rather than your friends." she said, looking at my confused expression.

I was shocked to hear that Mom knew almost everything about Abir—knowing that he had left for Canada and that I had gone on a date with him two days back as well.

"I know you have feelings for him. As parents, we have no problem with our children loving their lives or loving someone, but we just want you to be settled first. Because that is how we were conditioned. When I was married to your dad, I was a mere homemaker who had achieved nothing in life and since that day I have become a dependent woman onto your dad for everything. I don't want you to ever face this. That's why I was very strict about your career. But I am sorry; I too forgot that you have a life beyond the workplace as well. If you guys can strive for your love, you can strive for your career too." my mom said.

"Mom, you're not getting me. He has moved miles apart. It's like I just blinked, and he was gone." I cried.

"But he still remains close to your heart. Isn't that more than enough? I bet you recall the precious moments more than the stupid fights. When we lose a person, we barely care about the negatives of him.

"Fark sirf ess baat se padhta hai ki kaun tumhare dil ke kareeb hai.

Fer chahe uska ghar milo dur kyun na basa ho."

She smiled.

(What matters most is who lives in your heart than the distance physically in between.)

I hugged my mom and began telling her everything. She made me understand that it wasn't the right decision to hide the internship from Abir and that Kartik was just an obstacle that brought distance and misunderstandings between us. Later, I promised her that I would never fall weak and would share everything with her from that day. I apologized to her for misunderstanding her so many times and lying to her as well, but it was all out of fear. Probably, love could change things between us as well. I took an oath that only after I built a career would I consider getting back to Abir. Maybe months later, or a year, or even years.

"If it is meant to stay with us, it will. No matter what." I said.

8 MONTHS AHEAD...

Eight months had passed, and life had taken a different turn. Starting as an intern and now a full-time employee and team leader, I had worked hard to make my parents proud. My relationship with my mom had evolved too; we now enjoyed outings every Sunday, watching a movie, and having lunch together. She had grown fond of Riva as well, preparing a special meal whenever Riva stayed over. In these eight months, I hadn't spoken a word with Abir, but I continued wearing the pendant gifted by him every single day.

As March was ending this year, we got to know that Abir was returning to India.

"I want to meet him. But do I have the courage to go for it?"

"You should. He deserves to know that somebody waited for him for eight months." Mom said.

"What if he comes back with a new girlfriend? Must he not have dated someone there?" I got confused.

"You know him better. But why I want you to pour your heart out is to make you feel at ease, to make you feel free of all the emotions you have been holding for months. You need to give yourself a chance."

This is what my mom said that encouraged me to pour my feelings out. The surprising part was that I was in little touch with Abir's mom. She wished me on my birthday a few months back, and since then, we had our small talks. I decided to speak to her about him coming back home, to which she excitedly asked me to execute a welcome plan!

Chapter 16

Did it start?

I was feeling very scared. I took Riva along with me, and we booked a cake for his arrival. We moved to Abir's place where his mom greeted us warmly and asked us to wait for an hour until she returned. We thanked her, and she excitedly left with a smile.

"You know what, Riva, if there's something I regret the most about us getting separated, it is that I gave him so many grudges before he left, I broke his heart *twice*. And when I think of the last few days we had spent together, the only thing that comes to my mind is, '*Jab pata hai ki waqt kam hai, toh jitna hai, usse sahi se bita lena chahiye.*' (When you know that time is short, make the most of it)."

I rested my head on her shoulder, and she started consoling me. We waited for an hour, and finally, the bell rang. It was none other than Abir. I heard him coming upstairs and then opening the door knob. My heart started beating rapidly, and I started to shiver. I was getting butterflies in my stomach, and everything just stood still except for him. His jaw dropped as he saw both of us waiting for him inside his room. Riva blew the party popper and screamed, "A huge surprise for you!" He had his eyes wide open and tears shedding through his cheeks.

I couldn't wait any longer than we have already did. I broke his heart twice and shattered myself as well in the process. It's time to take what's mine, has been all along and will always be. My Abir. As he stepped closer, Riva hugged him and I kept on looking at him without an eye blink. His mom understood what was cooking between us and decided to leave with some excuse. I was silent, my lips not moving despite of me speaking of speeches in my head. My hands became stiff, despite of me longing to hug him and finally me eyes constantly making an eye-contact despite of knowing that YES, I WAS INSANELY IN LOVE WITH HIM.

Riva raised an eyebrow at me, asking me to begin with the speech.

"I have practiced a lot for this, so please don't you dare interrupt me. I know I made things terrible for you before leaving. I barely understood the love you had for me or the hints you had been giving me for years. But! The silly me has become a little more mature now. These eight months have indeed made me financially independent, but emotionally even more dependent on you. You rule my nights, you rule my days, and my overthinking never ends because of you.

"It was you who fell in love with me first. But it is going to be me who will love you till your last." I sighed.

After a moment of pause, he broke the silence by saying,

"You still wear this pendant?"

"It was a gift from someone special. That special left but his things still remain safe with me." I smiled.

"You chose to let that special go." He interrupted.

"Abir, listen to me. Ananya never entertained Ankush after you left. In fact, in the mall itself, she cleared everything with Ankush and Kartik. She told them how much she loved you and also gave the required closure to Ankush. That was the last conversation she has had with them! And she quitted the institute as well. She was scared when you mentioned that you would leave everything aside if she says a yes! Ana had no wronmg intentions, she just didn't want you to stop in the middle of your career because of her. That's what we do when we are in love right?" Riva jumped in between.

"I just wanted you to leave for Canada. I got scared that if in case I chose to confess my feelings, I might have won you, but it would have sacrificed your dreams. I was not prepared for that. You told me that you would not go if I said yes, how could I stop you from achieving something that you have always dreamt of?" I managed to say, my voice cracking with the weight of my emotions. It was hard to form the words, harder still to fight back the tears. Abir looked at me, his eyes reflecting a mix of regret, sadness, and determination.

"Ananya, I wanted to hear you, say it. But I also knew that it wouldn't be fair to you, to tie you down to my dreams. And love isn't about holding someone back; it's about setting them free."

His words tore at my heart. I had loved him for so long, yet our love had been tested and strained by circumstances beyond our control.

"It doesn't make it any easier." I said my voice barely above a whisper.

"I know, I've replayed that conversation in my mind a thousand times. But past is always bitter, right?"

We stood there in the quiet room, the weight of unsaid words hanging heavily in the air. There was so much left to say, so much left unsaid.

He broke the silence by questioning me why I didn't come to the airport to see him off. I told him that I had no guts to see him leaving. I was not accustomed to him leaving me in the worst of times. Above that, the guilt in me was breaking me to pieces.

"Because of what you guys did as best friends, the whole trio suffered. But I guess we need to make amends now. There is something that Ana wants to confess, and you have to listen to her." Riva interrupted, encouraging me to bare my soul.

I took a deep breath, gathering the strength to share what had been weighing on my heart for so long. "I loved you, but now I am IN LOVE with you. And I promise to love you, and to stay IN LOVE with you forever. I don't know if you still have feelings for me. So... Could you answer this puzzle for me?"

Abir's face contorted with a mixture of surprise, regret, and sadness. It was clear that my confession had impacted him deeply. He looked at me with an intensity that made my heart ache with longing.

I became silent and looked straight into his eyes. My heart was expecting a yes, but I was wrong. He just nodded and hugged me, and that was when my soul was torn. I had no words to say and that silence was just kicking me in. *He doesn't love me anymore.* Why would he? I broke his heart again, I distanced him myself, I am the one who destroyed this. I deserve this. He deserves all the love from the right person who will value him more than their life.

"I should leave." I said, picking up my bag and wiping my tears. I asked Riva to accompany me as well.

Before I could reach the door, he stopped me and said,

"Jin duriyo se, nazdikiyaan badhne lage, Woh duriyaan bhi behad khubsurat lagti hai."

(If the distance increases the closeness, the distance also seems to be bliss.)

Did I just hear lines of my book? The one I wrote?

"Where did you read these lines?" I asked, surprised.

"I moved to Canada, but that doesn't mean I forgot you or stopped keeping a check on you. I purchased your book the very first day it got listed on E-platforms. I knew the story was about us, and who could be more thankful than me who got the main character vibes while reading the entire novel! You surprised me, Ana. How did you do this?"

"After a month you left, Saloni ma'am contacted me for the Anthology competition. She motivated me to at least give it a try, and therefore one of the attempts led me to publish a wholesome book. And you know what? It's currently ranking 1 in our library. Although it's not an anthology book, the fictional novel made a great entry among others." I explained.

"I am proud to be called the best friend of a well-known author." Riva smiled at me.

"Ana, there is no concept like unloving somebody. If you ever unlove someone, it means you have never loved them at first place. So never in this life time assume that I stopped feeling for you because I still do, and I would do always. You

wrote an entire book on me and you think I could stop feeling for you? Stupid." With this, he kissed my forehead.

"So, more than just friends?" Abir held my hand.

"Well, that's the title of my book!"

"I know, but I am asking you the same. Will you be 'more than just a friend' to me?"

The biggest smile rocked on my face after months and before I could yes, his lips captured mine in the sweetest kiss of the kisses making me weak in the bones and if it wasn't for him holding me, I would have fallen straight on the floor. I got my happily ever after, my Abir, my love and best-friend in one person, what more could I have wished for? We kissed and kissed and when it was time to take a breath, he touched his forehead to mine, silently promising his love. We held each other for all the lost time and *yes you guessed it,* kissed some more.

And that's how we never remained 'just friends' after...

Acknowledgement

Disease! Sounds painful, right? At first, it did to me as well. But there's something intriguing about how illness often leads me to write a book. In 2020, while suffering from jaundice, I wrote my first book, 'The Midnight Boyfriend.' During the second wave of the pandemic Covid-19 in 2021, I published 'The Replicated Past.' Now it's 2024, and after undergoing foot surgery, I'm still healing, and once again, I've found myself with a new book.

It sounds quite amazing, doesn't it?

However, it would be unfair to begin this book without acknowledging Karandeep Singh Oberoi. He is the one person more invested in my books than I am. Without his encouragement and gentle pressure, I might never have completed this part of my life. Thank you, Karandeep.

About the author:

As a daydreamer, I often find myself lost in my own world, conjuring up fictional tales and intricately weaving them together, incorporating every fragment to bolster my imagery and imagination.

The journey of writing and publishing this book has been a profoundly enriching one, brimming with motivation, enthusiasm, and a surge of creativity. In my professional capacity, I guide high school students as a tutor, with psychology being the cornerstone of my career. Currently pursuing my master's in psychology, I find that this academic pursuit amplifies my creative abilities.

I ardently hold on to my dreams, diligently striving to bring them to fruition while effectively juggling the demands of work, my career aspirations, and a fulfilling social life.

"MORE THAN JUST FRIENDS?" is far more than a mere story to me; it's a part of my being, infused into these words, aspiring to resonate with a part of you.

Other Books:

The Midnight boyfriend

The replicated past

About the editor

This is Niharika. I am an English graduate, currently pursuing Masters and an aspiring Lecturer. I am a sucker for YA romance and fantasy. I love not only reading, but also to edit and review them. The novel held me captive because of the female protagonist that is reflecting the youth exactly as it is and I read it in one go. The plot is well-woven and will keep you in it's clutches. Needless to say, romance readers do love a great bestfriends to lovers romance anyhow and this is one of them. That's it about me, hope you enjoy the novel. ❤

www.ingramcontent.com/pod-product-compliance
Lightning Source LLC
LaVergne TN
LVHW041947070526
838199LV00051BA/2936